BURNED

SILVER WOOD COVEN BOOK NINE

By Hazel Hunter

D1176931

CHAPTER ONE

SNOW CRUNCHED UNDER Michael Charbon's bare feet as he walked through an endless forest of enormous gray-barked maples. Still slumbering through the last weeks of winter, the massive trees and their frost-veiled branches formed a canopied walk that led to an old sugarhouse. Michael breathed in deeply, letting the frigid air fill his lungs, and smiling when it didn't make him cold. He felt warm all over, which he also understood. The icy air and the frozen ground didn't chill him because it wasn't real. Somewhere else he lay sleeping with his mates in a warm bed. Everything around him was nothing more than a dream.

Michael.

As he reached for the latch of the weathered wooden door, Michael grinned. Inside he knew he'd find his mates: Summer Lautner, his beautiful witch lover, and Troy Atwater, his dark warlock brother. Troy was using the telepathic connection they shared as Summer's sentinels to call to him. Or were they sharing this dream with him now? He hoped so. They had been at odds with each other for far too long.

Michael, can you hear me?

Troy could be so impatient. Reckless, too. Since traveling to Canada to claim the two estates Summer had inherited, there had been too much contention between them. Here at Douce Lune Farm things had finally come to a head, but that had allowed them to end the rift tearing the three of them apart. Whatever coming challenges they had to face, Michael felt sure they would do it as a triad: three made one.

Wake up, Paladin.

The latch vanished, and then the sugarhouse and the forest dwindled as darkness swamped Michael. Something clamped over his face like a mask of smothering wool, and his nose and lips felt like ice. He wanted to touch his face, but his arms would not move. They seemed cold and numb, and he could not feel his hands at all. Slowly he realized he had awakened, and his entire body had been immobilized. Whatever had been done it had also dulled all of his senses, and slowed his heart to a weak, sluggish pulse. He felt no malevolent magic working on him, but a strange need to laugh bubbled up in his chest.

We've been drugged, Troy thought to him, *and Summer is gone.*

Knowing someone had taken their Beauty made Michael fight through the numbing haze and bizarre hilarity gripping him. He tried to take a deep breath, but his lungs filled with hot, acrid smoke instead of air, and he choked. As his body jerked, for the first time Michael felt the steel chains binding his wrists up over his head.

You have to hold your breath, Paladin. Troy's thoughts came into his mind like a rush of cool, calming water. *The farmhouse is on fire. Break the chains imprisoning us. Use your Wiccan power.*

Michael coughed out the last of the smoke and tried again to use his hands and arms, but they were useless. Anger roared inside him, but he clamped down on it in order to send his thoughts to Troy.

I cannot. My ability controls stone, not metal.

Steel is made from iron and carbon. Troy sounded odd, as if he were about to laugh out loud. *Carbon is made from coal. Focus on that. Remove it from the chains.*

What his sentinel brother asked seemed impossible. Michael didn't have the same control over his power than Troy had over his elemental ability with water. Yet if he didn't free them, they might burn to death, as fire was one of the few ways to kill immortal Wiccans. Not breathing made his lungs burn, and his head spin, but Michael drew on his love for Summer as he summoned his power, and poured it into the chains.

The links grew hot as they rattled and twisted, and then an amber glow illuminated the bed. Pain racked Michael, who thought for a moment that his arms would pop out of their sockets. In his desperation he prayed to the eternal Mother who watched over them all: *Goddess, please, help me free us, so that we might save her.*

Michael's power took on a blinding white corona, and the chains shattered.

As the walls sprouted flames, Troy sat up and held out his shaking hands toward the bath. Water came flooding out in a wide stream that splashed over them and the bed before rushing out to douse the fires around them. Michael untangled himself and staggered to the door, nearly falling down as the water rushed around him and streamed downstairs.

As soon as the flames were extinguished Troy directed streams toward the windows, freezing them into icy spears that smashed through the glass. Smoke wafted out, and cold, clear air rushed in.

"Beauty," Michael gasped as soon as he could take in a breath. The compulsion to laugh seized him again.

"He took her," Troy wheezed, as he gripped his shoulder. "Look at me."

When Michael did he muttered a spell that made him shake and double over. He coughed out a moist cloud of sharp-smelling gas. Troy did the same.

"It's still in the air," Troy gasped.

Michael stumbled over to the bed, shoving it aside as he picked up a large, hissing canister. He dragged Troy over to the window and flung the canister through it.

"Nitrous oxide combined with a sedative," Michael said.

"How the devil do you know that?" the dark warlock demanded, and heaved in the cold, clean air.

Michael didn't want to tell him, but his brother had to know who and what they were facing.

"Templars use it on powerful Wiccans they

wish to capture alive."

"Summer," Troy breathed.

"Us they were content to burn to death. Another Templar favorite." Michael paused. "But how could they have found us? No one knew we were here."

Fierce blue eyes narrowed. "Lorena did."

Michael didn't want to believe that the High Priestess of Artemis Coven would have betrayed them to the Templars who had been hunting Summer. Yet she had come to the farm to try to seduce him, which he had resisted. He'd also used force to make her leave. Even so, he shook his head.

"If she called Malveaux, he would have sent a team."

"Get us some clothes," Troy said and headed for the door.

While the dark warlock went to extinguish the last of the flames downstairs, Michael collected what dry clothing he could find. He imagined Summer in the Montreal Priory, surrounded by angry Templars determined to learn the location of the oldest and most powerful grimoire in existence, the Emerald Tablet. What none of them knew was Summer possessed all the knowledge of that ancient spell book, locked away in her mind.

Michael's own emotions faded as he drew on the remote, dispassionate focus that had kept him alive through Holy Crusades and Saracen prisons. He would find their Beauty, and then he would kill the one who had taken her. This monster had set his last fire. After Michael yanked on his clothes he brought some to Troy, who showed him a broken bottle that smelled of petrol.

"He used a Molotov cocktail to start the blaze."

If they still had a chance to rescue their Beauty before the Templars harmed her, then they had to go now.

"Get our coats and the bag of weapons from the closet," Michael said.

Once they were outside in front of the farmhouse, a strange glow on the horizon confused him. It was still too early for sunrise. Then Marcel, the farm's manager, came rushing from the back of the property, his gray hair standing on end as he shouted in French.

Troy ran out. "Did he hurt them?"

"No," Michael said and stared at the wall of flames and billowing smoke marching toward the farmhouse. "He set fire to the maple groves."

CHAPTER TWO

THE SMELL OF sweat, fear and petrol roused Summer Lautner from a drugged sleep into semi-consciousness. She lay on frozen ground. Her hands and ankles were bound behind her. Her only injuries seemed to be a stinging patch on her upper arm, and a scrape on her chin. She wore a strange and overly large set of camouflage pants and a shirt, and a wide strip of tape had been plastered over her mouth.

Slowly she opened her eyes to slits and let her pupils adjust to the darkness. Someone had left her in a field surrounded by trees and some old outbuildings. Moonlight showed her the silhouette of an ancient tractor nestled in icy weeds. A few yards away a dead tree rose from a clot of brown brush to claw at the sky with its grey, barren branches.

Another lurked nearby, beyond what she could see. She could feel the furious, malevolent presence as if it were a thousand hungry spiders dragging their fangs against her skin.

Michael and Troy!

She tried to reach out to them with her thoughts, but the drugs still tainting her blood made it impossible. Or had her abductor killed her mates?

No, I would feel it. I would die from it.

Just as Summer tried to summon the Emerald Tablet, heavy footsteps hurried toward her.

"Summer," a harsh voice whispered. "Don't make a sound."

It was Ally Martel, Lorena Paquet's bodyguard. Since Ally didn't know Summer had been gagged she obviously wasn't the abductor.

"It's all right, he's gone," the other woman told her as she worked on the knots. "I came to the farm to talk to you. I had to wait until Lorena was asleep. When I saw him carry you out of the house, I hid, and then I followed him. I don't know why he just dumped you here."

Summer suddenly knew precisely why. She was still smelling petrol, and began making muffled, urgent noises.

"It's okay," Ally said, and reached around to

peel away the tape. "I can get you out, my car is just over there." She peeled the tape away. "Did he hurt you?"

"He hasn't left," Summer gasped. "He's still–"

A shot rang out, and Ally stiffened against her. Then she toppled backward.

"Summer," she gasped. "My arm…"

Summer fought against her bonds as a shadow loomed over them. The moonlight slithered over the man's voluminous cloak.

"Finally, someone I can hurt," he said, his voice cold and flat. "Stand up, you snooping cow."

Gripping her bleeding arm, Ally struggled to her feet.

"My coven is on the way here," she said. "They'll arrive any minute, and then you'll have to deal with thirteen of us. You'd better leave while you still can."

"Ally," Summer murmured as she shifted up onto her knees, gritting her teeth as she tried again to summon her power. "Run, now."

"I wouldn't," the man said, as he leveled a gun at Ally's face. "If you do, I will shoot you in the back. Imagine life as a paraplegic." He pointed at the dead tree. "Over there. Back against the trunk."

Ally trudged slowly to the spot, her face shiny

with perspiration as she pressed her shoulders against the tree.

"You will pay for what you've done, Bûcher," she said.

The man laughed with genuine pleasure. "Is that who you think I am? How delightful, but wrong. So very wrong." As he kept the gun trained on her, he produced a pair of handcuffs. He tossed them to her. "Snap these over your wrists. Tightly, if you please."

When she had, he unsheathed a dagger from his belt. As though he'd wielded a blade every day of his life, he deftly lunged forward, caught the links of the cuffs, and lifted them high in the air. Ally cried out as her damaged arm was wrenched over her head, where he plunged the dagger into the tree. She dangled from it, on her tip toes, and began to murmur under her breath.

"Let's not resort to spells now," the man said as he stripped off one glove and stuffed it in the witch's mouth. He then stepped back and inspected her. "Yes, I think that will do. When I burn every night in my dreams I'm not nearly so comfortable. I go to Hell, where I'm first tormented by Lucifer's worst demons. Sometimes they impale me and slowly roast me over a pit. Other nights they chase me like a deer and shoot flaming arrows at me. I have been boiled in oil and thrust into a furnace and dropped by inches into a pit of lava. I feel every moment of the pain as if it is actually happening to me."

"That's why you've been setting these fires?" Summer asked, trying to draw his attention to her. "Because of your nightmares?"

"Because of your mother," he said. He strode over to stare down at her from the impenetrable black of the hood's deep cowling. "Before that fucking demon bitch and her sycophants died, she cursed me and my men. Each time we fall asleep, we dream of enduring our worst fear." He took out a matchbook and peeled off a match. "So every night, dear Genevieve, I burn in Hell."

"You killed my parents."

"I obeyed my orders, and destroyed the enemy," he corrected. "I am—I was—a soldier. That was my job." He struck the match, used it to light all the others, then pitched the flaming matchbook over his shoulder. "Now it's become a surprisingly enjoyable hobby."

The matches landed at Ally's feet, where they ignited the petrol-soaked dry brush around her. The witch screamed around the glove gagging her, and jerked at her cuffed hands, but couldn't free herself from the dagger.

"Please," Summer begged. "She's done nothing to you. Don't do this to her."

"She has only to endure it once," the killer said as he jerked Summer to her feet. "Look at her. Watch her burn, and you will understand what your mother's curse does to me every single night."

Unable to summon the Tablet's power, Summer focused her ability on the blazing tree, trying to turn it green again and stop it from burning. New branches began to pop out, and the flames died down. But Ally's clothes had caught fire, and she writhed as they burned away.

Please, do something to end this, Summer pleaded with the Tablet. *No one should die this way.*

But there was no answer.

As Ally's hair caught fire, the killer laughed.

"Stop!" Summer screamed. "Please!"

But as Ally thrashed and twisted, Summer knew there was only one thing she could do. Her stomach plummeted at the thought. Just then the dry brush erupted into an inferno so hot, that Summer had to flinch away. Beyond the wall of churning flames, Ally was burning.

"Goddess, forgive me," Summer muttered and threw all her remaining power into the tree.

A huge branch erupted from Ally's chest,

making her jerk. For a seemingly endless moment their eyes met—Ally's gaze strange and calm. Then she sagged and went still as the flames engulfed her.

Summer shuddered violently as tears slipped down her face.

"I should have left you to burn with your heathen lovers," the killer said. He seized Summer by the arms, and then released her with a sharp yelp. "Remove this spell from me," he roared, "or by all that is holy I will give you to the Templars."

Summer staggered, her ankles still bound, trying to see his face.

"Go back to Hell, you monster."

But as she tried to get closer, her toe caught on a bulging root. She pitched forward, unable to break her fall, landing hard and hitting her head. Her vision dimmed.

"Not this time, Witch," he said, as blackness swallowed her whole. "It is your turn to burn."

CHAPTER THREE

DRIVING AT NIGHT in rural Quebec might be the very definition of a dark journey. Theo could not see anything but what the headlights of his big RV illuminated. For most of the trip the view was comprised of empty, tree-lined roads, hilly snowdrifts and icicle-festooned wire fencing. What animals inhabited the area had, unlike him, the good sense to stay curled up in their shelters.

"Is that fog?" Raelyn Foss asked, peering through the windshield of the RV.

A dull cloud appeared to be rushing toward them.

"It's steam," Theo told her, switching on the wipers. "Troy diverted a river to try to save the farm's trees."

The young woman made a soft, mournful sound as they passed a grove of smoldering, blackened maples.

"I don't think it worked. Why would someone want to burn a farm?"

"It was one of the old ways of defeating an enemy," he told her. "Burn the crops and lay waste to the land, and the people starve. But this is more malicious than strategic. This farm was left to Summer by her father, Jean-Paul. It was all she had left of him."

"Maybe it wasn't just being cruel. It could be payback." Raelyn sat back and used her Wiccan ability to shift her appearance, changing her hair and eye color to black. "Maybe someone took everything from him, and it makes him feel better to see someone suffer the same way. I mean, if it's not Summer who did it to him first."

"The lady would never want anyone to suffer, I think." He gave her a sharp look. "Do you know someone who does?"

She shrugged. "It happens a lot in foster care. The kids you live with don't let you get away with anything. You mess with them, and they make you pay for it."

Theo suspected she wasn't being entirely honest, but they had arrived at the entry gates of Douce Lune. He drove up to the front of the house, where Troy stood talking to several worried-looking mortals.

"Stay here," he told Raelyn.

Outside the air felt warm and damp but still smelled of burning wood. The front of the farmhouse showed signs that it had also been attacked by the arsonist. He went over to the smashed front window, saw the ruins of the room inside, and muttered a vicious curse in the oldest language he knew.

"I agree," Troy said as he joined him. His handsome face was grim as he touched Theo's broad shoulder. "Thank you for coming right away."

"I wish I'd arrived sooner. I would have enjoyed catching this demon and sending him to the Hell he so obviously misses." He saw the mortals retreat around the farmhouse. "Where is Michael?"

As if in answer to his question a black SUV pulled up, and the big man climbed out. His expression as he walked over to them was that of a furious beast on a badly-fraying tether.

"Hello, General. I fear we need your help most urgently." He glanced at the scorched groves to the east of the house and his jaw tightened. "How much was lost?"

"Marcel says about a third," Troy said. "But

without the river water, it would have been all of them. They'll take it from here." Troy turned to Theo. "We have to get to Montreal."

"The area is swarming with police and emergency units," Theo noted. "We were one of the last vehicles to make it over the bridge."

"The bridge?" Troy said, scowling. "But why…" He paused and then grimaced. "The river."

"The surge alarmed more than a few of the higher-ups," Theo said. "They've erred on the side of caution."

"How do we get across?" Troy asked.

"Leave that to me, my boy," Theo said, and gestured at the RV. "Put your things in there and ride with us. Michael, follow us in the car, if you would."

Raelyn helped Troy stow the weapons bag in one of the RV's cloaked cache spaces, and gave up her front seat so the two men could talk. As the dark warlock provided more details on the attack, Theo drove as fast as his mobile home would allow.

"Michael is operating in full warrior mode," Troy added after he finished the grim tale. "Don't get between him and this guy. He'll stomp over you without a second thought."

"I surmised as much when I saw his face." A thought occurred to him. "Troy, have you attempted to access Summer's thoughts?"

Troy nodded. "We both did, several times, but she doesn't respond. Michael thinks he gave her an extra dose of sedation. He found an empty syringe by our bed."

"Keep trying to link with your lady. I believe whatever drug he employed will dissipate more quickly than he calculated." As they drew close to the police barricade blocking entry to the bridge he slowed to a stop. "Raelyn, my sweet, would you fetch for me that rather important-looking envelope marked 'PMO', please?" To Troy he said, "Try to look grumpy and superior, like your father. That's the way. A few more wrinkles and some silver hair, and you'd be his twin." Once Raelyn handed him the envelope, he grinned. "Thank you, lovely girl."

Theo lowered his window for the approaching officer. He wore a lieutenant's insignia in four yellow stripes on his shoulder epaulettes.

"The bridge is closed. You must turn around and divert to the north."

Theo offered up the envelope. "You should read this."

As the lieutenant read, he gradually came to

attention.

"The vehicle just behind is with me," Theo said, as the lieutenant returned the envelope.

"Yes, sir," the man said crisply.

A few moments later the lieutenant began directing his men to move the barricades aside, and Theo closed his window.

"So what was in the envelope?" Raelyn asked as he drove onto the bridge. "Some please-me-officer compulsion spell?"

"There is no such thing," he told her firmly. "PMO stands for Prime Minister's Office, and the letter in the envelope grants me virtually unlimited privileges while traveling in Canada, thanks to that lovely young man they just elected to office. Ever the champion of the underdog, I understand."

Troy's dark brows arched. "You don't know the prime minister."

"Alas, I do not," Theo conceded, "but my old friend, the retired PM, stole a vast quantity of the official letterhead before he left office."

At the other end of the bridge he employed his counterfeit letter again to pass through the second road block, and then drove to the nearest deserted spot he could find.

"I must take Raelyn to the safe house before I join your search for Summer," Theo told Troy as they walked over to meet Michael, who spun the car around before he stopped. "I'll call you from there."

The big man rolled down the passenger window and peered at them through it.

"Troy, the news radio channel reported an explosion in Westmount."

"Meet us at the overlook," Troy said to Theo as he jumped in the SUV.

As Summer's mates drove off, he detached the Jeep from the RV's trailer hitch. Though Raelyn watched, she remained unusually silent. As he drove her to the Magus Corps sanctuary, however, he could feel her seething temper as if it were steam wafting from her ears. Finally the dam burst.

"Why can't I go with you? I know I stole the RV but I've behaved since then. I've done everything you've asked me to without bitching. I could help. I can shift into a man if I have to. I can make them think I'm a Templar."

"You are still mortal," he said gently, "and not yet fully recovered from the memory sickness. The Templars are now using bombs, and you can be easily killed. Until that changes, my sweet girl, you cannot help."

She made a frustrated sound. "You could have

changed me the other night."

Theo let her stew until he reached the safe house, where he shut off the Jeep's engine and turned to her.

"I wanted to change you the other night. I wanted to strip you naked and pleasure you and bring you into eternity. In all the centuries I have walked this earth—and there have been many—I have never wanted anything or anyone as much as you."

Tears shimmered in her eyes. "Then why didn't you?"

"There is a reason I must wait. A selfish one, I fear." He reached out to touch her cheek. "I am in love with you, Raelyn Foss. I do not merely wish to bed you. I want you as my mate. My wife. For that, you must be a woman full grown."

Her eyes shifted from dark brown to pale gold as she lifted one trembling hand to her throat.

"Did you just propose to me, Theo?"

"Not yet," he said and leaned forward to cradle her face between his large hands. "But the moment you are well, my darling chameleon, the very second you can truly choose, I will be on my knee before you." He touched his brow to hers. "While we wait until that wonderful day, we must be friends. So, be a good girl and do this for me."

Raelyn leaned forward and stole a kiss from him. "I love you, too."

The long-suffering captain on duty at the safe house agreed to guard Raelyn until Theo could come back for her. After they'd settled her in her room, and Theo bid her goodbye, the captain walked him back to his Jeep.

"You've brought me a Templar, and a color-changing mortal," the captain said. "What's next, General? A dragon in need of wing repair?"

"Never that," Theo assured him. "I hate dragons." He bid the captain lean closer, which the man did. "But when I do return, I will find Ms. Foss healthy, happy, and sound. If I do not, you will drink molten gold. I will pour it down your throat until it rises in your eyes—just before I turn it to pins." He cocked his head at the captain who stiffened to attention. "Do we understand each other, Captain?"

The captain saluted. "Yes, General!"

CHAPTER FOUR

MEN MOVED LIKE dark ghosts around the abandoned train yard that served as the public face of the *Prieuré de Montreal*. Patrol teams marched along the perimeter, while guards flanked the entrances to every building. Because Dr. Salomon Tolbert had ordered that the Temple Master be carried into his quarters, rumors circulated just as busily.

Add to that the fact that his steward, Bastien Berger, had been taken to the hospital in a coma. None of the garrison had stepped forward to confess to the boy's savage beating, though the doctor felt sure he could name the assailant.

In Massimo Malveaux's bed chamber, which occupied a large corner of the yardmaster's office, Salomon finished dressing the Temple Master's extensive wounds. The stink of blood and antiseptic blended unpleasantly with the wounded man's cologne, but the doctor didn't mind. Salomon had smelled much worse on the battlefield.

"There are questions I should ask, judging by the substantial scarring you already have," he said as he taped down the last layer of bandages. "Such as, who did this to you, were photographs taken, and how long have you been indulging in recreational flagellation?" He drew the sheet up over Massimo's ruined back. "But if you wish to have your body whipped to shreds, and expose yourself to ridicule or infamy, or both, I think that is your business."

The Temple Master opened his wet eyes and stared at the wall behind Salomon.

"Your discretion is appreciated, Doctor," he said, his tone listless. "You may go now."

"We will talk a little more before I do," the doctor said. He checked Massimo's pulse and adjusted the blood pressure cuff. "As an immortal Templar you do not age, you heal quickly, and you are not easily killed. That said, the amount of punishment you can subject yourself to is not infinite. Blood loss weakens you. Some of your wounds were to the bone. If you are not careful, these pain games you play may go too far someday. Do you understand me?"

"As you say, it is not your business. But I thank you for your concern." Massimo pushed himself up from the bed, clenching his teeth as he stood, and ripped off the blood pressure cuff. "Bring me my clothes."

"They are soaked with your blood," Salomon said, and brought a light robe and helped him slip it on. "There is another urgent matter we must discuss. Genevieve Lautner."

"I know," Massimo said, moving stiffly as he tied the robe. "My men destroyed her manor in Westmount, so she will run."

Salomon nodded. "How did you discover where the witch was living?"

A smirk ruined the perfect line of Massimo's mouth. "The woman who scourges me is a witch. When she beats me, she also rants about those who anger her, like Lautner. I employ a blood spell to coax her into revealing such things, and then forgetting that she did. All she remembers is how she punishes me."

"You use heathen magic and deviant sex to obtain information?" Salomon demanded. "How can you live with yourself?"

"I pay the price for it, I assure you. But that too has its rewards." Massimo smoothed a wrinkle out of his sleeve. "The moment the Lautner woman tries to leave Montreal, we will have her. Then the Emerald Tablet will be mine, and you–"

"We already have Lautner in custody, Temple Master."

Massimo stared aghast at him, to which Salomon only nodded and looked away.

"Someone dropped her outside the gates," the doctor added. "She was discovered bound and unconscious when the guard was changing."

The temple master quickly hobbled over to his armoire. "Where is she?"

Salomon wondered if the Temple Master had even the slightest conception of how much trouble he was in.

"Peyton took her to your dungeon for interrogation, which I would like to conduct. This young woman has information about the arsonist. I am convinced of it."

"The last time I asked you to aid us with an interrogation, you told me that you were a doctor, not a torturer," Massimo reminded him as he took out a suit and shirt, and placed them on his bed. "Besides, I wish to question her myself. Jeffrey will assist me."

"You are in no condition for that," Salomon advised him. "Under the circumstances, you will permit me to interrogate the witch."

The Temple Master eyed him. "Or?"

Salomon squinted back. "I will see to it that every man in the Priory knows that you frequent places like Club Chaînes where you allow sadistic women to beat you for your sexual pleasure." Salomon took out his phone and showed him the variety of pictures he had taken of Massimo donning a mask as he entered the fetish club, and the full gory extent of his most recent injuries. "What is it that you call yourself when some mortal female is abusing and humiliating you? Bûcher?"

Massimo's lips went white. "How dare you."

"Don't even think it," he added as the other man took a step toward him. "I have made copies and entrusted them to an old friend. If anything happens to me, they will be sent to your men and the Grand Master in Rome. How long do you think it will take him to decide to remove you from Montreal and revoke your membership in the order? Two minutes? One?"

"You didn't come here to vacation," the Temple Master said, spitting the words like oaths. "You were sent by Rome to ruin me, weren't you?"

"I have absolutely no interest in you, Massimo," Salomon assured him. "But I will question this witch—alone. Once I am finished, you may do with her whatever you wish."

CHAPTER FIVE

THE PARKING LOT of the Westmount lookout was lit by a single dim light. Though the stars above them shone a milky path to the western horizon, the three men in front of their vehicles only had eyes for the scene below.

Troy slowly lowered the binoculars. "Beaumont Manor is gone," he said tightly. He handed the lenses to Michael. "It's nothing but rubble and ash."

In the distance below, the swarm of emergency vehicles was breaking up. From the lookout, they could see the surreal scene lit by cycling red beacons and the beams of headlights. But there was no question about the explosion that had been reported. It had leveled Christien Beaumont's estate.

"First the farm," Theo said from behind them.

"And now this," Troy said through clenched teeth.

As Michael lowered the binoculars, they creaked in his big hands, just before they snapped.

"It was an all out attack," he said, his normally deep voice strained. He tore the binoculars apart and flung them to the ground. "Why do we wait, Brother?"

"Correct me, if I'm wrong," Theo said, staring at the broken halves on the ground. "But you don't know where your lady is."

"It has to be the Montreal Priory who is responsible," Michael said, seething. "Everything about this bears the stamp of Templars."

"The train yard is their stronghold," Troy added. "That's where they would take her."

"The train yard," Theo said flatly. "Ah yes. I understand you two know it well."

Troy glared down at him. "We're wasting time."

Michael started toward the SUV but, impossibly, Theo stepped in front of him.

"Will you dig another collapsing tunnel?"

The big man barely managed to stop from running the dwarf over.

"Your courage does you credit," Michael growled with thinly veiled menace. "But it will not save you from a thrashing."

Troy jumped between them. Michael had been pushed too far, something Troy knew from painful experience. But Theo wasn't the most feared and powerful warlock in the Magus Corps for no reason. Putting a hand in the middle of Michael's chest, Troy turned to his diminutive friend.

"If you have something up your short sleeve, old friend. Now is the time to pull it out."

Theo's eyes blazed. It was a look that Troy knew well. Though his friend no longer served in the Magus Corps, the man was a warrior through and through.

Theo nodded. "That's the first intelligent thing you've said this night."

"Brother," Michael growled. Troy felt the rage beneath the word. The big man spoke slowly. "Beauty has been taken. Who knows what they are doing to her this very moment."

Troy took a deep breath and took his hand from his brother's chest. As always, his mate's words cut to the crux. He grimaced as he looked him in the eye.

"I know," was all Troy could say. He turned back to Theo. "Hurry."

"The wisest course," the warlock said, "is to call for reinforcements." When Michael bridled, he held up his hands. "Wisest, though not necessarily the best." A keen look came over his mentor's face. "We have two tactical advantages. First, they think the two of you are dead. Second, they think they've won." The dwarf regarded him. "Think, dear boy. I know I taught you better than that. Use that battle-hardened head of yours."

Although Troy frowned at him, his words began to sink in.

"Their guard will be down," he said, then shook his head. "But the element of surprise will only go so far.

"The priory is still heavily fortified," Michael agreed, calming down a fraction.

"Of course," Theo said. "Of course. Three warlocks will not make a frontal attack." Troy noted the number three. "No. You've tried to sneak in, and you've tried to tunnel in. You must try a different way."

Troy's mind churned over the possibilities. Although the Templars had just razed the manor and torched the farm, the three of them didn't have the luxury of returning the favor. Summer was still inside the stronghold. Even so, there was something about fighting fire with fire that had a vengeful appeal. The ensuing chaos was the perfect opportunity for a small team to take advantage.

Troy looked behind him at the view from the overlook, not really seeing it as an idea began to form. Finally he turned back to Theo and Michael, and slowly he grinned. Before Michael could ask, Troy sent him the plan through their mind link.

The big man's eyes narrowed. "You really think it could work?"

"Of course it will work," Theo said, his voice brimming with confidence. Though he'd yet to hear a word of the plan still solidifying in Troy's mind, the short warlock smiled broadly. "Because that is how I taught him."

CHAPTER SIX

SUMMER OPENED HER eyes and looked up at a rough ceiling cornered by dusty cobwebs. It took a long moment before she remembered falling in the pasture. Ally was dead, and the killer had brought her here, wherever that was. She couldn't sense him anywhere near, but that meant nothing.

As her head throbbed miserably Summer tried again to contact her mates. But it was as though her mind were wrapped with a drug-induced gauze. Only a strange, muffled silence pervaded. Resigned, she inspected her surroundings.

She lay on her side, gagged, with her hands bound behind her. Iron bars formed a large cage around her, which had been lit with bright white fluorescent lights. The only furnishing was a metal chair that had been bolted to the center of the floor. The cell had not been cleaned for a very long time, and was so cold she could see her own breath on the air. Machinery and crates had been piled by the walls outside the bars, and a dank, murky smell in the air made her guess she was underground, where sounds would be muffled. From the claw marks and rusty brown stains on the concrete floor of her cell she guessed the prisoners before her had screamed often and loudly.

Shoes scraped across the concrete, and Summer closed her eyes.

"I know you are awake," a harsh male voice said. Keys jangled in a lock, and a big man opened the door to her cage and walked in, locking it behind him. "On your feet, now."

That was when Summer realized her feet were no longer bound. She used her elbows to push herself up from the floor to her knees. From there, she managed to stand on slightly wobbly legs.

The man standing before her looked too big and bulky to be the killer. He wore camouflage fatigues, similar to her own. His short haircut and the clothes suggested he was military, but she could sense his immortality now. Her throat tightened as she recalled what the killer had said just before she'd blacked out.

It is your turn to burn.

He'd delivered her to the Templars.

"My name is Jeffrey Peyton," the man said. His tone didn't change, and he looked at her as he might a snake ready to strike. "I am the Temple Master's lead investigator. All I wish to do is speak with you." He reached out and pulled down her gag. "Do not attempt to use your witchery."

Summer said nothing. Templar cop or not, she didn't trust him, and she'd use whatever it took to escape. She suspected he knew that, too.

Peyton took a step back, but the tension in his body and knotting of his muscles indicated he was fully prepared to lunge at her.

"Do you know who left you here at the priory?"

If she didn't answer him, he might start hurting her.

"No," she said. "He concealed his face."

He gestured at the chair. "Sit." When she didn't move he looked up at the ceiling and then at her. "Do you wish to provoke me to violence? In the state I am in it will take no more than a prod, girl."

Summer sat down slowly.

"This is against my better judgment. I should

kill you for what your mother did to me." Some
of the hard lines around his mouth eased away.
"But without you I may never know peace again."

Summer felt dread bloom inside her. The
arsonist had also blamed her mother for
something she'd done. Was this the reason Marie
had gone into seclusion with Jean-Paul and
Christien?

"What do you want?" she asked, keeping her
expression blank.

"The man who brought you here," he said
carefully, "did he tell you that he was cursed by
your mother?"

She could lie and say no, but she saw no point
in it.

"Yes."

Instantly Peyton's entire demeanor shifted from
angry to furious. He swore in archaic French as he
paced the length of the cell. He dragged his big
hand over his sweating face. He looked at
Summer as if he wanted to strangle her. Finally he
stopped and crouched down in front of her,
folding his hands tightly.

Somehow Summer knew he was trying to keep
himself from punching her, which made as much
sense as the rest of his bizarre behavior. Yet the
fear in his eyes appeared very real, and if he had

wanted to hurt her he would have already started. She decided to trust her instincts.

"You said my mother did something to you. What was it?"

"I was there the day Marie Lautner died," he said. He sounded completely unrepentant, simply a soldier who had performed his duty. "An informant told us where she was hiding, and my team was sent to capture her."

This was another of the men responsible for destroying her family, Summer thought dully. She blinked hard before she asked her next question.

"What do you want from me?"

"For you to know that I did not murder her," he said. He lowered himself the rest of the way, sitting on the floor in front of her, his eyes staring past her shoulder. "Our orders were to bring her back alive for questioning. But her men would not surrender. They were killed along with three of our men. We were not told that their deaths would end Marie's life as well." He trembled all over as his gaze shifted to her face. "Do you believe me?"

Summer studied his features, which looked haggard. The shakiness, the bags under his eyes and blood-shot condition of his corneas suggested that he had been awake for days.

"Why do you care what I think?"

His jaw worked for a moment. "Because I am going mad, girl, and if you are as powerful as they say…I need your help."

"My name is Summer," she said. The despair in his voice almost made her feel sorry for him. "Tell me what happened to you."

In halting words Peyton described how, with her last breath, Marie had cursed him and the surviving men on his team. The curse was as the killer described: nightly, horrific dreams in which they had to endure their worst fear.

"I have tried everything," he said, and leaned back against the bars. "Drugs and drink don't stop the nightmares. Nothing does. I did not know the others shared the curse until Diego Velasco, one of the other men who was there, confided in me. He told me he dreamt of being buried alive and slowly eaten by insects, over and over, every night. He had himself beaten unconscious but even that did not stop the nightmares from coming. Eventually it drove him mad, and he drowned himself in the sea."

Summer felt sick. She knew the Templars killed her parents, and her mother had been dying when she cast the curse, but what Marie had done seemed horribly cruel. It was also the sort of malicious magic that her parents had despised, and to Summer's knowledge had never used.

"The arsonist told me that he was cursed, too. He burns in Hell every night. Which one was he?"

"I cannot tell you. Except for Velasco I never learned what the others suffered in their dreams. They all left the priory and scattered to seek a cure." He met her gaze. "You helped Gaston Moulin, Lady Summer, so I know you can be merciful, even to an enemy. If you will tell me how to end this curse, I will release you, and see to it that you escape the priory."

So she was at the Montreal Priory, the Templar stronghold. Even if she could contact her men, what would they be able to do? The real possibility of her dying sank home, and yet this Templar was offering her freedom. It didn't make sense.

"Why not just torture it out of me?"

"I considered that," he said, as his knuckles whitened. "But I am a man of faith. I do not believe in suicide. If you should die before you gave me the cure, I would be damned to suffer for eternity." He swallowed hard. "Or I would go mad, as this arsonist has."

His brutal honesty made Summer think of Gideon, the Templar who had gone insane from immortality sickness. Along the way he had become a vicious rapist, and later had maimed or killed nearly every mortal who had crossed his path.

"Do you remember what my mother said when she cast the curse on you?"

"She spoke of you, her daughter, and all the suffering we had caused you," Peyton said. "She said we would know the same." He shook his head. "I can never forget her eyes in that moment. They glowed like emeralds on fire."

Summer felt confused. She knew the spell, which was a mirroring curse. Marie had branded her with one variation that caused the harm intended to be reflected back on any attacker. But the Templars hadn't attacked her mother.

A thought occurred to her, one so terrible and cold that it twisted inside her like a blade of ice. A verdant power awoke and expanded inside her mind.

"What did my mother's voice sound like when she cursed you? Did she speak in English?"

"Like that of an old woman," the Templar said. "She spoke in ancient French. I was the only one who understood her." Peyton frowned. "Why?"

"Give me a moment, please."

Summer closed her eyes, blocking out

everything but the entity seething inside her.

You cursed these men.

I avenged the murders of my Guardian and her sentinel mates, the Emerald Tablet said in its old crone voice. *Marie suffered nightmares every time she slept. She refused to use our power, and grew weak and helpless because of it. Now they but enjoy the same torture.*

Summer held onto her temper with a death grip. If her mother had cast the curse, she would be unable to remove it from Peyton. Since the Tablet had cast the spell through Marie, however, they could still release the Templar from it.

End this man's suffering, now, or you and I are finished.

He will not keep his word.

Summer opened her eyes, and knew she had to do something to keep Peyton from giving into his murderous impulses. She extended her arms.

"I will need my hands free to do this."

Peyton looked suspicious as he took out a blade. Once he cut through the cords he sheathed the knife and took in a deep breath.

"I am hung naked by my heels," he said, his eyes unfocused. "It makes the blood rush to the head and keeps me alive while the saw men work."

Summer blinked. "I beg your pardon?"

"The sawing torture. It is my worst fear. I was only a boy when I saw it done on Crusade to a captured Saracen." His mouth took on a bitter curl. "Every night in my dreams I am hung upside down, and sawn in half, vertically, from my balls to the top of my skull. The saw men are careful to avoid the spine so that every cutting stroke is felt. They do their work slowly. Sometimes they stop part the way, and do other things, like piss in my face, or make use of my mouth."

Bile surged in Summer's throat, and she swallowed hard before she reached for his hands, and gripped them.

"Look at me, Jeffrey Peyton." Once she had locked his gaze with hers, she drew on the Tablet's power. "I forgive you for the harm you did to my family."

To the Tablet, she thought, *Now you will forgive him, and end this grotesque curse.*

Who are you to command me, Daughter? The entity demanded.

I am the Guardian, she thought back. *We agreed. I contain you, and you empower me.*

You have never wished for my power. By ignoring me you cast me to slumber, and our concord grows weak and distant. Soon it will be as it was with your mother. You will try to summon me, but I will be too deep in my dreams to hear you…until it is too late.

Summer rushed through her memories of her mother as she tried to recall ever seeing Marie use the Tablet's power. All she could remember was her fathers casting spells for her.

If I don't use your power, you go to sleep. If I let you sleep long enough, I won't be able to wake you again. Why didn't you just tell me this?

Why didn't you ask? the Tablet countered. *There is no containing or empowering. You were born to serve me, but I exist to serve you. We share the same soul, Daughter.*

She felt a little shaken by that revelation, but quickly recovered. *Then you know how I feel about what has been done to Jeffrey Peyton. He helped take my parents from me. If I can forgive him, so can you. Will you break the curse you put on this man?*

As an answer the entity poured energy through her and into Peyton. *Damned as you deserved, and cursed with nightly horror, full punishment has been served, no more shall you dream in terror. The spell I break and your mind I free, for my Daughter's sake, so may it be.*

The power of the Tablet enveloped the Templar, who stiffened and cried out. Thin streams of black liquid poured out of his eyes, nose and mouth. The dark fluid splashed on the concrete and sizzled like acid before it evaporated into the green light. Peyton collapsed, shuddering feverishly as he slumped to the floor.

For a few moments, he lay still, but then his eyes opened. Though still underlined by thick, dark circles, they were no longer haunted. He sat up and shook his head a little, as though he were testing it.

"I feel...I feel myself again," he said, his voice thick with emotion. He peered up at her, tears glittering in his eyes. "It's over now, isn't it?"

As the tears began to stream down his weary face, she turned away to hide her own.

"Yes."

"Thank you," he said, his voice choking. "Tonight—"

A klaxon sounded in the distance, strident and blaring. Somewhere up above a door slammed as well. Men shouted, the panic clear in their voices.

"What's going on?" Summer asked.

Peyton scrambled to his feet, unlocked the cell door, and grabbed her hand.

"That's the fire alarm. Come on!"

• • • • •

"Where is the fire?" Massimo demanded.

"I don't know, my lord," said the Templar guard

as he ushered him out. "But we must evacuate."

• • • • •

Dr. Tolbert rushed out into the quad, only to be confronted by pandemonium. Dawn had only begun to steal across the sky, but the interior of the train yard was awash with light. The rotating red beacons of two enormous fire trucks, three paramedic vans, and two squad cars bounced crazily off every surface. Uniformed men of every variety were dashing to the various buildings.

An explosion made Salomon duck his head. A column of flames erupted from behind one of the old fuel tanks.

"Are those empty?" yelled a big man in coveralls and a helmet.

He was pointing at the tanks, but looking at Salomon. The doctor was about to say he didn't know, when a second explosion detonated. The man ran past him, followed by two fireman dragging a hose.

"Get away from the tanks," the big man yelled as he waved his hands. "Get away from the tanks."

To Salomon, that seemed like good advice.

CHAPTER SEVEN

WITH TROY BEHIND him, Michael ran in the direction of the dungeons. Courtesy of the Westmount hardware store, they wore coveralls trimmed with reflective tape, construction site helmets, and work boots. While Troy carried a fire extinguisher, Michael had opted for an ax.

Theo should have one more Molotov cocktail, Troy thought to him.

The building where they held Gaston is there, Michael thought back. He pointed with the ax.

The plan had been shockingly simple. All three of them had called Montreal emergency services and reported an enormous blaze in the train yard. The old rail ties were burning out of control. The fuel tanks had never been emptied. They'd waited outside the gates until the panicked sentries opened the iron doors and the firetrucks drove through them. Theo waited outside the wall, near the tanks.

Michael hurtled past Templars, keeping the rim of his helmet low. He yanked open the door to the building where Gaston had been, nearly tearing it off its hinges, and charged into the dank interior. The dungeons were below. Once they got low enough, he'd use his Wiccan power and start moving through them one at a time. He would tear it apart stone by stone to find his Beauty.

Two fleeing Templars ran up the dark stairs toward them. Michael gripped his ax in both hands, but Troy gripped his arm.

Get in and get out, Troy thought to him.

"Right," Michael muttered.

But the second of the Templars abruptly came to a stop and turned.

"Michael?" said the familiar voice. "Troy!"

It was either the smallest Templar in existence or—

She reached up to her head, and ripped off the camouflage shirt that she'd used as a bandana.

"*Beauty*," Michael said.

"Lord and Lady, thank you," Troy murmured, and swept her up with one arm.

Michael grabbed the two of them, almost picking them up off the ground. But before he could utter his thanks, the first Templar turned around. In an instant, Michael had Troy and Beauty behind him and had raised the ax.

"No!" Summer said. "He helped me to escape. He–"

The last Molotov cocktail went off.

"There's no time for explanations," Troy said. "Summer, wrap your hair back up." He reached for Troy's ax. "Brother, put her over your shoulder."

"Gladly," Michael said, wasting no time.

He bent before her as she finished with her hair, then he lifted her familiar weight with ease. The nameless Templar, who wore camouflage pants and a t-shirt, stood aside. But as he and Troy passed him, Michael nodded, and the man solemnly nodded back.

Out in the yard the chaos had only worsened. Two long arcs of water were assaulting the old fuel tanks. Troy led the way as they ran past the fire trucks, out the massive iron gates, and down the narrow sidewalk. Michael gripped his precious package, trying not to bounce her. As they rounded the corner the Jeep came into view. A short arm stuck out from the driver's window. It waved them forward.

CHAPTER EIGHT

SUMMER FELT HERSELF being settled down onto something. When she could look around she realized it was the back seat of the Jeep. Two car doors slammed.

"We're in," Troy said. "Let's go."

The tires squealed as they took off, and Troy pulled her onto his lap. As he wrapped his arms around her, Michael leaned over and buried his face in her chest. Their three-way hug was awkward, but as Summer shut her eyes, she had never felt anything so good in all her life. She lay against Troy's hard chest and hugged Michael's strong neck, as joy and relief and wonder mixed inside her. For several long moments there were no words, only the tight clasp of arms and hands.

But as the Jeep sped through the streets of Montreal, Summer realized she smelled smoke.

When Michael raised his head and looked all over her face, his jade green eyes were underlined with sooty smudges. Troy's worried forehead was smeared black as well.

"Are you all right, love?" he asked.

"Did they hurt you?" Michael said.

She thought of the arsonist and how she'd been knocked unconscious, but then she remembered Ally.

"No," she said quietly, ignoring the knot on the side of her head. "I'm fine." But she was seriously smelling smoke. "Did you really start a fire?"

Her mates exchanged a long look before Troy held her left hand, and Michael clasped her right. Summer didn't have to open her mind to them to know something was terribly wrong.

"He set fire to the farmhouse, didn't he?" Summer said. "Before he took me away."

"We saved the house," Troy told her. "And about two-thirds of the maple groves." He hesitated, but then plunged on. "We didn't hear about Beaumont until we came after you. The Templars used an incendiary bomb–"

"The manor is gone," Michael said gently. "We are so sorry, Beauty."

Summer dragged in a breath as she tried to process just how much she'd lost. But the thought of the manor being gone didn't disturb her as much as what the arsonist might have done.

"Was anyone at the farm hurt, or killed? Renee and Marcel?"

"They're fine, love. So is everyone else at the farm." Her dark warlock lifted her cold hand to his lips. "The only damage done was to us, and your legacy."

"Not just us," she said, and leaned her head against his shoulder. "Ally Martel saw him take me from the farm, and followed him into a trap. I was the bait."

As she told them the rest of it, she wondered why her voice sounded so strange, and then realized she was sobbing the words.

Troy cradled her head against his shoulder.

"Theo, drive to Artemis House. We must warn the coven." To Summer he said, "The arsonist. Is he a member of the Montreal Priory?"

"He was one of the Templars who killed my parents. I don't know what he is now, other than a monster."

She mopped up her tears with the edge of her sleeve and watched the first pale, rays of daylight illuminate the horizon.

Theo paused the Jeep at a stoplight, and adjusted the rearview mirror to look at them.

"My welcome at the coven will be little better than at the priory," he said. "I'll wait in–"

An enormous boom shook the air, vibrating through the SUV. Summer gripped Troy tightly, as all four of them peered out the front windshield. A column of dark smoke poured up into the air a block ahead of them. As Theo turned down a side street, they saw the ruins of Artemis House.

Shattered glass littered the streets and sidewalks around the old building, and flames and smoke filled the windows. Injured women staggered out of the first floor entry, clutching each other and looking dazed. More coven members leaned out of the upper level windows to shout for help.

Theo parked in the alley behind the coven house and climbed out.

"I know the way," he said.

"I'll deal with the fire," Troy told Michael. "You clear the rubble and get the women out. Summer–"

"I'm going in with him," she said. "If the building starts to collapse, he'll need me."

The dark warlock's mouth flattened, but he nodded. "Be careful."

Michael and Theo led the way through the clouds of smoke and dust into the shattered building. As Theo pointed, the big man used his strength and Wiccan power to move aside the mountains of rubble blocking the staircase. Water came streaming in around them to put out the smaller fires, and then raced up the walls to seep into the upper levels.

On the second floor they found no one alive, but discovered several women trapped in an elevator stuck on the third floor. Once Michael pried open the doors Summer pulled each woman out and directed them to follow Theo downstairs.

The last casualty they found was Lorena's mother, Fabiola Paquet, pinned beneath a heavy statue of Diana in a spell-casting chamber. As Michael lifted the sculpture away, the old woman opened her eyes and squinted at Summer.

"Marie? Have you finally come back?" She coughed, and blood trickled from the side of her mouth. "Lorena is so hurt. She cries for her Papa every night, but he will not come. I do not know what to do with the girl. But the cards do not lie. The Goddess promised us, Marie."

"I am Genevieve, Madam," Summer said gently. "Marie's daughter."

She glanced at Michael, who was checking the massive wound in the old woman's abdomen. He looked up and shook his head.

"Is Lorena here now?" Summer asked.

"That mad Templar took her," she said. The old lady's eyes sharpened and focused on Summer's face. "He stole her and the old grimoire she took from you. She intended to use it to steal your power, child. I tried to reason with her, but she did not listen. She is obsessed, and more dangerous than you can imagine."

"Lorena couldn't steal my power," Summer told her. "Guardians are born to it, not made."

"My daughter should have been a Guardian," she said, as the color drained from her face. "I can't feel my legs anymore. It's rather nice after so many years of pain." Fabiola coughed and shivered. "Why is it so cold in here? Didn't we start a fire in the hearth?"

Michael took her hand and rubbed it lightly between his.

"This will be warmer, *cherie*."

"You are very kind for a Templar," she whispered. Her chin wobbled. "When I am gone, will you take me out to the country, and bury me there? Somewhere it is always in the light? I hate the dark. I always have."

"It would be my honor," Michael assured her.

Summer was about to take her other hand when the dying woman seized hers and gripped it tightly.

"What is it, Madam?" Summer said.

"I remember now," Fabiola gasped. "Say you will forgive me, Genevieve. Please. Do not let me die with this on my conscience. The Goddess was wrong. *I* was wrong."

"You have done nothing to me," Summer said, and felt the gnarled hand go limp.

Michael reached over to close the old woman's eyes. "She is gone."

CHAPTER NINE

ONCE THEY ASSURED that everyone who had survived the explosion had gotten out of Artemis House, Summer finally had a chance to catch her breath. Almost in a daze, she watched Theo direct small groups of witches away from the building and off into adjoining neighborhoods. From there, they would be escorted by Magus Corps officers to safety. The faint sound of sirens could be heard in the distance.

Troy suggested they leave Montreal at once.

"The Templars will be out combing the streets for Summer, and I think we need some time to rest and decide what to do next." He watched Michael gently place Fabiola Paquet's body in the back of the Jeep. "We also need to bury Madam Paquet as she requested." The dark warlock frowned at Michael, apparently sharing his thoughts. "I was thinking more like a five-star hotel in Toronto."

Summer struggled to focus on the conversation. "I know a little bed and breakfast in Quebec City."

"Malveaux will still have men watching the roads," Troy said.

"I believe a dwarf driving an RV might get past them," Theo said, returning.

"Thank you for your continued help, old friend," Troy said, resting a hand on his shoulder.

An hour later they had collected the RV and then Raelyn from the safe house. With Wiccan covens exploding, Theo had decided she was safer with him. At a travel plaza, amid transport and moving trucks, the diminutive warlock filled up the tank for the motorhome and the Jeep. Then he and Raelyn stopped in at an adjoining coffee shop, and brought back muffins, pastries, and hot coffee. The five of them ate in the comfort and privacy of the RV.

Summer sat with Raelyn and listened as the men discussed the Templar attacks, and reasons as to why the arsonist had abducted Lorena instead of killing her at the coven house.

"This madman is not behaving like a Templar,"

Theo said as he offered Raelyn half of his blueberry muffin. "He's far too vicious. They would never tolerate the potential exposure. What perplexes me is that he delivered Summer to the priory. If he desired her to be tortured, why not do it himself?"

"Perhaps he tried while she was unconscious, and failed," Michael put in. "With the spell brands protecting her, he would not have been able to torture her for long."

"That may also be the reason he took Lorena," Troy said slowly. "He may think he can use her to find us. Or she may be using her emotional web to make him suffer." He grimaced at Raelyn. "Sorry for the reminder."

"No, it's okay," the young woman said. But she got up and collected the empty cups and wrappers. "Summer, would you mind grabbing the trash bag out of the kitchen? I'd like to drop it in that bin outside before we leave."

Summer collected the bag, but as soon as they left the RV she saw how Raelyn was looking at her.

"Is there something you want to tell me that the guys can't hear?"

"The High Priestess, she makes you want her," the young woman said. "I'm not gay, you know, or into older people, but as soon as I joined the coven I fell for Lorena. Or at least I thought I did. She messes with your mind."

They dumped the trash and Summer dusted off her hands.

"She tried that on me, too, the day I interrupted that session she was having with you. I have two men who keep me very busy in that department, but Lorena used her power to arouse me…and it worked. I simply said no."

Raelyn thrust her hands in her jacket pockets.

"I couldn't. Say no, I mean. Every time she came at me I just…let her. I never had anyone want me like that, so I guess I was flattered. It's stupid, I know." She ducked her head. "There's something that happened that's still fuzzy, but I'm getting flashes of it now. Lorena hurt me because I found something in her chamber. I can't remember exactly what, but she kept it hidden in an old trunk."

"Don't try and force the memory. It will return on its own. I speak from experience." She smiled at the young woman. "Was that all you wanted to tell me?"

Raelyn blushed. "I did want to ask your advice on something. Now that I finally found Theo, a guy I genuinely want, he won't, you know, do it with me. He says I'm too young, but do you think it's something else?"

She wasn't yet twenty, Summer reminded herself.

"No, it's definitely the age difference, honey."

"Yeah, I thought so," Raelyn said. She kicked a stone on the ground. "He says we have to wait. But I feel like if I don't do something about it, I'm going to be a mortal for the rest of my life."

"Seeing just how much Theo loves you, I seriously doubt that," Summer said and slipped her arm through Raelyn's. "It's worth waiting for, so that's what I think you should do. The right guy plus the right time equals pure magic. I also speak from experience on that one, times two."

"He proposed, you know. Well, sort of." Raelyn made a face. "But there's this waiting thing."

"But it's respectful, Raelyn," Summer pointed out. "Theo knows how you feel, and he's still insisting on this. In a way it's for you. He's courting you. He's showing you that you deserve to be respected. I'm guessing that hasn't happened too often in your life."

"No, but really?" The girl looked doubtful. "I never think of how old he is. I just lust after him. I mean, have you seen his chest?" She held out her hands like she was describing a fish she'd caught. "You could play football on his pecs."

"Keep lusting after it, as much as you like," Summer said as they crossed the parking lot. "Because for a while that's all he's going to let you do."

For the dangerous trip out of Montreal, Theo drove as usual, and Raelyn took the front passenger seat. Troy, Michael and Summer retreated to the RV's back bedroom, where the exhausted trio dropped on the bed. Nestling between their bodies felt like a living fortress stood between her and the rest of the world. She'd be perfectly happy never to get out of bed again, too, if it meant they'd be safe.

"I found out some other things about my mother," she told them, her eyelids already heavy. "Things we need to discuss."

"I'm ready," Troy said, stretching and yawning, as Michael rubbed her back.

"It's just that the Emerald Tablet told me something very odd," she said as she slipped her arm under Troy's. "We share the same soul. Obviously I was born with mine. I don't think it has one of its own because it was a book, not a living creature. Of course it was a tree first—but not a person." She yawned, and then so did Michael. "Maybe it created the Guardian bloodline so it could be more like a person. You know, have a body, and move around. Trees must envy us that way."

"Beauty," Michael murmured. "Go to sleep."

Summer looked at Troy, who had already drifted off, and sighed. "Okay."

CHAPTER TEN

A GRASSY TRAIL lined with golden rose bushes and dark violet plum trees spiraled out before Summer. Tiny hummingbirds darted from bloom to branch. The vivid colors of their red, amber and green tiny heads and the deep blue of their bodies made them seem like jewels that had taken wing. Mist dampened the air, capturing and concentrating the deep, lush scent of the roses. Silver dew speckled the dusky skins of the ripe plums, which hung low, ready to be picked.

Michael appeared beside her, his open white shirt exposing the hard plane of his brawny chest. In his hand he held one of the golden roses.

"So, Beauty, you finally went to sleep."

She chuckled. "I believe I did. Do you know where we are?"

"A dream garden," Troy said, and came out

from behind one of the trees, plucking a plum as he did. "Someone else is here, too." He nodded at the end of the trail, where a majestic oak tree had been planted.

Summer's smile faded as she began walking toward the physical manifestation of the Emerald Tablet. Her mates flanked her and kept pace until she stopped a short distance from the massive oak.

This creature, if it could be called that, had been the cause of every sorrow Summer had ever known. She had never wanted its power, and still resented that she had been given no choice but to become its Guardian. Yet it had also given her Michael and Troy, the two greatest gifts in her life.

"Why have you brought us here?"

The path began to spin, and Summer's men grabbed her as the landscape shifted around them. The roses and plums changed into the flowers and hedges of Marie Lautner's estate garden.

Summer gasped as she saw Jean-Paul Dechamps standing on a ladder. The big, golden-haired man snipped away with trimmers at the very top of a towering topiary. Her heart clenched as she recognized it. Her golden father had always shaped it for her like an enormous rabbit standing up on its hind legs and holding a basket. Whenever she came home to visit, she always found a present from Jean-Paul inside the basket, too.

Christien Beaumont came out of the house carrying a tray with coffee, fruit and bread, which he set down on the patio table before he unfolded a copy of a *Le Journal de Montréal*, his favorite newspaper.

"Come and have breakfast," he called in French to Jean-Paul.

As her golden father climbed down from the ladder, Michael suddenly stiffened.

"What is it?" Summer asked.

He nodded toward the high stone wall at the back of the garden, where something glinted. A man lowered a pair of binoculars and smirked before he dropped down out of sight on the other side of the wall.

Marie appeared, dressed in a silk floral robe, and smothered a yawn as she sat down with her mates.

"Good morning," she said. She kissed both men before she poured the coffee, but shook her head when Christien offered her some fruit. "I am not hungry, *mon cher*."

"You are growing very thin," Jean-Paul said.

"Come now. You know that Genevieve will be safe with our friends in America. It is why you sent her away. You must stop worrying about her."

"It is all I can do," Marie said as her mouth turned down. "I have tried and tried to summon the power. It is buried so deep now I think I will never be able to use it again."

Summer saw Christien lift his newspaper from the table, and spotted the date printed on the front page. She knew exactly what day in the past that they were watching. Turning her back on her parents, she glared at the tree.

"I don't want to see any more of this. Stop it."

Marie and her lovers froze as a curtain of green light surrounded Summer and her mates. A crudely-carved doll appeared from behind the tree, and walked stiffly up to her. It had to tilt its pointed head back to gaze up at her with the dark charcoal smudges that served as its eyes. Fashioned out of green wood, it had a small log for its torso, and twigs for its arms and legs, but no mouth. A familiar, rasping voice came from it.

"You wished to know which of the men has now gone mad and is burning pagans," it said. "I will show him to you."

"By making me watch my parents die? No,"

Summer said flatly. "Take us back."

Marie's garden spun around them again as flames blazed through the flowers and mortars exploded. When it stopped Summer saw her battered, bloodied mother crawling toward the motionless, bullet-ridden bodies of her mates.

"They're gone," said a grim-faced Jeffrey Peyton, who tried to pull Marie up from the ground. "You're coming with us."

Another man with an eyepatch and bald head kicked Marie in the face, making Summer flinch. Her mother sprawled across her lovers' bodies.

"Why do you always talk to them, Peyton?" the one-eyed Templar said. He chuckled as he looked down, revealing a thick red scar at the top of his head. "You have only to carry them if you knock them out."

Summer wanted to bury her face against Troy's chest, but she forced herself to watch as Marie wept over Jean-Paul and Christien. The ghastly tableau froze again as the wooden doll appeared, and lifted its twig arms toward Summer, like a child wanting to be picked up. She wiped her eyes before she bent and took hold of the doll, lifting it up and propping it on her hip.

Michael nodded at the short man with the eye-patch. "That is the one we seek."

"He has lost his mind, but not his wits," said the doll. "He is the most dangerous enemy you have." The doll turned its head toward Troy. "Elemental, you must stay close to the Guardian, and all three of you must take care. He will come for Genevieve again. If he uses drugs, we now know I cannot stop him."

The burning mansion and garden whirled around them until they returned to the garden of roses and plums. The doll and the tree were gone, and Summer sank down on the grass beside her mates. While she knew the Tablet only meant to help, it had no mother. It would never be human. While it might share her soul, it could not feel pain, or horror, or regret.

Troy put his arm around her. "It's all right, love. We're here, and we're not letting you out of our sight again." He kissed her brow. "Unless that weird doll comes back."

"Then we may run away, very fast," Michael said, caressing her cheek. "I think there will be some screaming, too."

She tried to smile at their lighthearted quips, but couldn't quite manage to do it.

"Sorry, love," Troy said quietly.

"As am I," Michael said. "Since we were brought together we have been constantly besieged by horror and hatred and death—and now sinister dolls that scare Beauty and make me angry." His broad shoulders slumped. "It is almost as bad as being a Templar witch hunter."

"Oh, no, Michael." Summer touched his arm. "It can never be that bad again. Troy and I won't let it."

"We've never surrendered to the hatred," Troy said, "and I'm not going to start now." He extended his hands to her and Michael. "With joy and love and life, we fight back. Together."

The big man gave him a long, silent look before he took his hand. "Always."

"I think it's time to start, now," Summer said, also taking his hand.

As the power of their triad flowed through them, she opened her mind to theirs. For the first time since she'd been taken, her lovers minds merged with hers. At first relief flooded through her. Then she felt their lingering sorrow and anger from what they had witnessed in her mother's garden. But the moment their emotions combined with her own, the love they shared flowed through it, adding courage and hope. New roses bloomed around them, their petals vivid blue with streaks of every color in the rainbow.

Their clothes melted away, leaving them naked

and gleaming with sunlight. Summer stroked her hands over the smooth skin and hard muscle of her mates' chests. She rolled her shoulders back to lift her tight-peaked breasts. Troy and Michael began kissing their way to her nipples, which they laved and sucked until she trembled with need.

Summer knew they weren't actually making love in the sunlight. Yet the touch of her lovers' hands felt incredibly real, and aroused her so quickly that she pushed Michael down onto his back, stretching out on top of his massive frame. The heat from his body sank into hers, fulfilling one half of her need.

"Troy," she whispered.

"I'm here, love."

Her dark warlock stroked her back as he knelt behind her, his swollen shaft resting against the cleft of her buttocks. He radiated his elemental coolness over her, which blended inside Summer with Michael's earthy warmth.

"Paladin," Troy said. "Let me take her first."

"Yes. Her sweet pussy is very wet." Michael looked into Summer's eyes, his own burning with desire. "You will make Troy's cock very slick."

"Oh," she gasped. Her eyelashes fluttered as she felt the dark warlock press between her folds, his swollen shaft stretching her as he pushed deep inside her wet, clenching pussy. "That feels so good. You're going to make me come too soon."

"Then we will make you come again," Michael said, and cupped her breasts, thumbing her nipples in time with Troy's slow strokes. "And again, and again."

"We need to give her more," Troy said.

He slid out of her, shifting as he reached between her thighs and gripped Michael's shaft, guiding it to her until the broad head lay lodged at her opening. He then shifted his hands to Summer's hips, and pressed her down. Michael grunted as she enveloped him, his muscles coiling and his lips parting.

"Now you, Brother," he said. He reached around Summer to fist Troy's gleaming girth, and positioned him at the tight ruck of her rosebud. "Fill her tight, lovely little ass."

Already impaled by Michael's hard cock, Summer shivered as Troy began to push gently into her bottom. The sensation of being filled twice surged through her, making her feel beautiful and hot, and pushed her to the very brink of bliss.

"Here I am, love," Troy groaned. He gave her the last inch of his shaft, and braced himself on his arms. "Michael and I are going to fuck you now."

The big man slid out of Summer's fluttering pussy, and when he pumped back in she felt Troy draw out of her ass. They alternated like that, working in and out in juxtaposition, making her writhe and cry out as the sweet friction became a sensual torture.

"We will not stop," Michael warned her, catching her chin and bring her mouth to his for a brief, hard kiss. "We will keep taking you every night. If I am not in you, Troy will be."

"You'll wake every morning covered in our kisses," the dark warlock said, "and creamy with our seed." He nuzzled her neck. "You'll come just thinking about the next time we take you."

Summer stiffened and heard herself scream as the sexy threat hurled her into a whirlwind of pleasure. She tumbled over and over, her body lighting up with the intense pulses of delight as the storm of passion smashed through her.

"That's it," Troy said, his voice low and hoarse as he steadily plowed in and out of her ass. "Give us everything, Summer. All of it, now. Michael, come."

Michael muttered something in French as he arched under her, his cock swelling and jetting deep in her pussy. Then it was Troy's turn to grunt and shake as he pumped his warm, wet seed into her tight channel. Summer groaned in protest as they both withdrew from her body, but as they rolled her onto her back and flanked her on each side she felt incredibly, impossibly content.

"You meant that?" she asked them. "Sex every night?"

"We are sorry about that," Michael told her. "But we cannot manage to have you every hour."

"Or we would," Troy assured her, making her chuckle.

Slowly the opal flowers and the rest of the garden faded to sepia, and Summer opened her eyes to find herself back in the RV's bed. Troy and Michael were clasping their hands, and held hers, just as they had in the dream. They looked at her with drowsy wonder.

No more walls between us, she thought, keeping her mind linked with theirs. *We are stronger together. Three made one.*

Her mates' voices blended together in a beautiful harmony as they repeated the triad vow. *Three made one.*

A knock on the door made Troy sit up before he called out, "Come in."

Theo opened the door enough to stick his large head inside.

"We made it out of the city," he said. "Michael, since this property of yours is to the north, and Raelyn and I must go south, I suggest we stop for a meal in Mirabel, and then part ways."

Theo glanced at the three of them, but without another word he closed the door.

Summer looked at Michael. "You own land in Canada?"

"No, Beauty," Michael said. "You do. Troy and Theo helped me make arrangements for the estate anonymously. We hired a construction company of Wiccan elementals to rebuild the mansion and restore the grounds. It was to be a surprise for you."

"But why would you…" Her eyes widened. "Whose estate was it, Paladin?"

"Your mother's," he said, smiling. He kissed her cheek. "Happy birthday, Beauty."

CHAPTER ELEVEN

LORENA TESTED THE cords binding her wrists and ankles, which had been knotted so tightly her fingers and toes had gone numb. Cockroaches skittered around her feet, and when she moved, rust flaked onto her from the crumbling strut to which she had been tied. The Templar didn't know it, but she had been conscious since he had dragged her out of his van and carried her into the factory. While she was concerned—a Templar gone insane was the most dangerous creature on the planet—she didn't feel overly alarmed.

In fact, she might be exactly where she needed to be.

From what she could see the Templar had hidden his lair in the center of the factory's cluttered, man-made warren. There he had set up a kind of command center, where he had covered one wall with monitors and cobbled together feeds from a dozen different desktops. Cables ran the length of the building from the makeshift array to a modified breakout box. One large desk held a street map of Montreal. Daggers had been stabbed into different locations.

In a chair beside the desk sat the bland-faced Templar himself, flipping through the pages of the possession grimoire she had stolen from Douce Lune farm. He muttered under his breath, moving his finger along one line of a spell written in a form of Latin devised by ancient Wiccans, the letters of which rearranged themselves randomly until subjected to a decoding spell.

Lorena smiled a little as he slammed the spell book shut and shoved it away, and then assumed a frightened expression as she cast out her psychic web. She tasted his madness—he was most definitely insane—but also sampled determination, fear, and the purest, cleanest rage she had ever absorbed. Her nipples puckered, and a gush of wetness soaked her panties as she wallowed in the power of his emotion, but only for a moment. Now was not the time for self-indulgence.

"My lord knight," she said softly, and when his

head snapped up she sent a warm wave of affection through the web to engulf him. "Why have you spared me?"

The Templar got up and walked over to her, his eyes crawling up and down her body before he clamped a hand around her throat.

"The Lautner witch has bespelled me. You will remove it."

That startled her, and she embraced him with her unseen web, using it to search out Summer's magic. She found instead an old-fashioned ward that had been transferred to him by touch. But then she found a dream curse so powerful and dark it burned her senses like acid. Quickly she retracted her web and assumed an appalled expression.

"You have been twice cursed," she lied. "Summer and her mother have worked terrible magic on you. You must be the strongest man on earth to endure such torment."

The compliment had no effect on him. "Remove the spells, now."

"I cannot do that," Lorena said. As he drew a dagger she added quickly, "The moment I cure you, you will kill me."

"Remove the spells," he repeated, pressing the tip of the blade under her right eye, "or you will be begging me for death every day until you do."

The danger aroused Lorena even more, and she poured her hot desire into the web, soaking him with her lust.

"Surely you can find something else to do with me."

The Templar slowly lowered the dagger, sheathing it before he shoved his trembling hand under her skirt. Once he clumsily jerked down her panties, he took out his large, erect penis and guided it to her.

"I'm going to rape you, Witch," he rasped.

The moment his cockhead touched her pussy, however, he moaned and shook. Lorena felt him spurt against her folds before he could penetrate her, and fed shame and humiliation into the web.

"You can't even fuck a helpless captive, you useless moron. Now do you see what Summer Lautner has done to you? How she has turned you into a miserable little worm?"

The Templar staggered backward, shoving his wilting member back into his trousers.

"Remove the spells," he pleaded. "I beg you."

Now she had him. "First you will release me." As he went around the strut and began fumbling with her cords, she licked her lips as she fed on his fear. Stopping before she had fully sated herself made her feel peevish, but the satisfaction that awaited her would be so much more delicious. "Then we will talk about what you will give me if I help you."

Once she was untied, the Templar came around to face her, cowering as she added more power to the web and spiked his fear.

"What do you want?" he whined. "I will do anything you ask." He knelt down in front of her. "Please, command me."

His abrupt submission proved too much for her to resist. Lorena dragged him over to the soiled pallet where he had been sleeping and shoved him down on it. A flick of her power made him go erect again, and she jerked his penis out of his pants and straddled him.

"Look at me," she said, slapping him when he kept his face averted. "This is how you fuck a helpless captive." She shoved herself down on him, until she gripped him to the root, and then tore open her blouse. "Squeeze my breasts. Harder. Make them hurt. Make me hurt."

Fucking the whining madman gave Lorena more pleasure than she had felt whipping Bûcher at Club Chaînes—with the added bonus of not having to wear a ridiculous disguise and call herself Madam Peine. As he timidly pawed her breasts she rode him hard, making the pallet slam over and over against the wall.

"You are my bitch now, Templar," she told him just before she allowed him to climax, and fed off his shocked pleasure as she milked his ejaculation with her internal muscles. "That's it, that's my good boy."

After Lorena came she straddled his face and made him clean her pussy with his tongue. Only then did she climb off the pallet.

"I am your Mistress now, Madman. I will teach you how to cast the spell that will transfer Summer's powers to me. Then all we have to do is set the trap, and lure her to us."

The Templar got up and hung his head. "Yes, Mistress."

"Get your car. We have work to do."

CHAPTER TWELVE

SUMMER DIRECTED MICHAEL to a protected nature preserve north of Mirabel, where they were able to find a secluded, sunny spot to bury Lorena's mother. Michael used his power to dig the deep grave for her remains, while Troy recited a beautiful Welsh poem about the soul's freedom after death. The big man gently placed Fabiola in the grave, and covered it over again.

Finally it was Summer's turn, and while she had never understood the old woman's hatred, she could still feel some compassion for her.

"For you there will be no more pain or suffering. Now you will know rest, and peace, forever." She bent down and touched the dirt covering the grave. "Good-bye, Fabiola Paquet."

Little seedlings began popping out of the soil,

uncurled and stretched up as new green leaves unfurled. A few minutes later the grave was covered with hundreds of dandelions blooming bright yellow in the sun.

After stopping to pick up some groceries, toiletries and new clothes, Summer and her mates continued the journey to her mother's rural estate. Knowing the Templars had burned her mother's mansion to the ground had always hurt her, as she had grown up there. Until she met Troy and Michael it had been the only home she had ever known. Now she would see it fully restored again. Without her parents there it would probably feel bittersweet, but having her childhood home returned to her would go a long way toward healing the old wounds.

Summer's first sight of the belvedere lookout that rose from the hipped roof made her smile. Christien had often taken her up to that little, glass-walled tower to bird-watch with him. Michael's contractor had replicated it exactly as it had been.

"We used to sit for hours and watch for golden eagles and nighthawks," she said. "Sometimes we'd see a boreal owl come out just after sunset."

Troy parked at the turnaround in front of the east wing, and once Michael helped her out he handed her a key.

"Theo's archivist was able to find the original house plans," Michael said as they walked up to the main house. "Since we had no photos of the interior, it was up to the designer."

The wide overhanging eaves had been painted a pristine white, while the walls of the house had been cased with smooth, light sandstone veneers. When Summer had lived here Marie had painted the eaves dark blue, and the walls an earthy amber. But if Michael had matched them, they would have felt depressing. To see her childhood home in different colors instead made it seem updated, and welcoming—an old friend in new clothes.

Inside the house every room looked different, of course. All of the furnishings, drapes and carpets were new and more modern in style. Yet somehow the designer had recaptured the classic ambience that her very French mother had adored, while giving the rooms an air of comfortable elegance.

Summer reached out to caress a bright pansy in one of the floral arrangements by the sitting room door, and laughed as she touched the wall instead. The *trompe l'oeil* painting of the bouquet had been detailed so realistically that it seemed as if real dew drops sparkled on the petals, and a tiny ladybug had just landed on one of the fern sprigs. The optical illusion had also been worked with a shadow beside it, precisely shaped like the flowers, which gave it the three-dimensional trick that so thoroughly fooled the eye.

"You'll have to stop giving me birthday presents," she told Michael. "You can never top this."

"Troy may have," he said and smiled at his sentinel brother. "Why don't you take her upstairs while I unload the car?"

The dark warlock offered her his arm, and walked with her up the curving, dark teak staircase to the second floor. Down the hall she saw the door to her old bedroom, but Troy steered her in the opposite direction.

"If something jumps out at me from my mother's spell chamber," she warned him, "I'm hurting you."

"It's a good surprise," he promised, and then stopped in front of the master bedroom.

For a moment Summer didn't want to look inside. She knew they couldn't reproduce the interior, but she didn't want to see the room changed to something else. Her parents' bedroom had always been the sanctuary of her childhood. As a little girl she had run countless times to jump on the big bed and wake her mother and fathers in the morning. Marie would chuckle and shake her head, Christien would grumble about the early hour, and Jean-Paul would tickle her unmercifully. She had also crept into their room when storms rumbled over the mansion, and the flashes of lightning seemed too close. Her mother would hold her and her fathers would murmur to her until she fell asleep, safe in their arms.

Troy reached out and opened the door, and Summer pressed her hand over her mouth. Everything looked exactly the same, down to the slightly faded Aubusson carpet on the floor, and the strings of prismatic crystals Marie had hung in the windows.

As tiny rainbows danced across the floor, Troy said, "You brought me and Michael into this room once, in a vision. We didn't stay very long…" He gave her a pointed look, reminding her that they had seen her parents about to make love. "But we both remembered how the room looked. It took a lot of internet searches and phone calls, but I found a bedroom set exactly like your mother's in an antique shop in Ontario."

Summer walked over and sat down on the edge of the bed, too overcome to speak. She touched the violet and gold satin coverlet her mother had so loved, and looked up at the matching canopy with its golden tassels.

"Michael had the bed linens custom made," Troy said. He came to join her and slipped an arm around her waist. "Did we take it too far?"

"It's perfect," she whispered. She quickly wiped away the tears threatening to spill. "It's just…so much has been taken from me. You and Michael have given me back something so precious and beautiful…" She stopped and shook her head.

Troy eased her back and held her, looking into her eyes as he told her how the interior designer had handled all the practical work, so they would never accidentally let her in on the surprise through their thoughts. The enormity of what her lovers had done finally sank in, and Summer sat up

"This house has two wings, and fifteen bedrooms, and a wine cellar and… Troy, how could you afford to rebuild it?"

"We did not pay for it, Beauty," Michael said as he came in carrying a bottle of wine and three glasses. "When you sent Nathaniel Harper and his men back in time, I still had access to the deserted New York priory. Before the Templars in other priories realized what had happened, I transferred their assets to an offshore account. Troy and I decided the money should be used to help their victims."

He set the glasses down on the nightstand and began pouring.

"Your name was first on the list," Troy tacked on.

Summer wasn't sure how she felt about that. She had despised the Templars who had stolen Michael from his Wiccan family and raised him to believe he was one of them. In her eyes their money was beyond filthy. But the order itself had killed her parents and destroyed her mother's estate, while Michael had saved her life, loved her without question and built this dream for her. Accepting it from him made it a gift.

"Can we sleep in here?" she asked tentatively. "Unless you think that would be really weird."

"This is your house," Troy reminded her. "We'll sleep wherever you want." He gazed around them. "I do like this room, though. They don't make beds like this anymore. It's big and sturdy enough for three. I like having an adjoining bath, and the fireplace is certainly romantic."

"We can toast marshmallows while we are naked," Michael said, and brought her a glass of wine. "A crackling fire always feels good on bare skin."

Troy rolled his eyes. "Maybe we should put some cushions and pillows on the floor in front of it now."

"Or we could sleep in your old room," Michael put in. "I looked at it when I came upstairs. It's very pretty." He glanced at Troy before he said, "Pagan thinks we might smash the little bed."

"That's because it's meant for one," Summer said and set aside her wine glass and theirs before she hugged them. "Thank you for this. I love you both so much."

CHAPTER THIRTEEN

EXPLORING HER NEW/old childhood home
filled several happy hours for Summer, and then
she made dinner for them in the large, spotless
kitchen. As a little girl she had learned to cook at
Marie's side in the old version, which had been a
sunny yellow with green-painted cabinets, and
white and gold marble counters. In the current
version, the contractor had installed the latest
appliances in stainless steel. The counters were
black granite, and the cabinets white pine, fronted
with glass. A black and white checkerboard
backsplash ran the length of the counters, and
bright red canisters and linens added a fun splash
of accent color.

Once Summer had plated the stir-fry and rice
she'd made, Michael helped her carry it out to the
dining room, where Troy was setting the polished

cherry wood table. She stopped to watch him, and imagined doing that for the rest of their lives. They could live here, far from all the turmoil and disaster, with nothing to do but take care of their home, make love, and raise their daughter. It seemed like heaven, but she knew her mother had not come here to have a simpler life. Summer recalled how much Fabiola had seemed to despise her, and yet had begged for her forgiveness just before she died.

"My mother left Artemis Coven just before she moved out here with my fathers," she said as she took a seat. "She made them abandon their homes, which they obviously both loved very much. Yet they did that willingly, and I never heard them say a word about it."

"It could not have been Templars," Michael said, spooning heaps of the steaming food onto his plate. "Even in their absence, they would have destroyed your fathers' homes."

Troy looked troubled. "But they came here instead."

"That's just it," Summer said. "We lived here for more than twenty-five years before they found my parents. Jeffrey Peyton told me an informant betrayed them. I think it might have been someone from Artemis. Maybe even Fabiola herself."

Michael shook his head. "Lorena and Ally were the only coven members who knew the location of Jean-Paul's farm."

"If Ally wanted you dead," Troy added, "She wouldn't have tried to rescue you from the killer."

"So it was Lorena," Summer said, as her appetite fled. She set down her fork. "If she betrayed us to the Templars, she might be the same informant who got my parents killed. But why? What did my mother and I ever do to her?"

"Since the killer abducted her, we may never know," Michael admitted.

"Don't be too sure of that," Troy warned. "With her ability to manipulate emotion, she could easily have survived."

"She is just as dangerous as the killer," Summer said. "We have to go back and find them, or more mortals will die."

Troy nodded. "But not tonight." He spooned some food onto her plate. "Eat."

Once they cleared the table, Summer went with her lovers for a look at her mother's gardens. The landscaping company had already planted most of the hardier bushes and plants, covering them with protective canvas until warmer temperatures arrived. She liked the addition of a new deck, and the rustic irregular slate tiles that formed the walkways through the beds. As the moon came out and illuminated everything with diffused silvery light, Summer bent down and removed one of the canvas covers to reveal the clusters of hydrangea flowers opening beneath it.

"The Summer effect still works, I see," Troy said as he crouched down beside her. "I wonder what you could do if you really tried."

Since waking from the garden dream in Theo's RV, Summer had not tried to call on the power of the Emerald Tablet. She still felt reluctant to use or rely on the entity. Yet from the memories it had shown her, she now knew that if she avoided it, she would lose the ability to summon it as her mother had.

"Why don't we find out?" she asked, and walked over to where Michael was inspecting a latticed arch over a wrought iron bench. "Come with us, Paladin."

She led her mates to the center intersection of all the walkways, where a new stone fountain had been installed. Water cascaded down tiers of green jasper carved to resemble lily pads, and bubbled from rose quartz flowers to splash in the broad basin. There she took hold of their hands, and closed her eyes as she summoned the Tablet.

You are not in danger, the old crone's voice snapped. *Why do you disturb me?*

I want to restore my mother's gardens, Summer thought back. *I thought you might like to help.*

The entity flowed through her as it merged with Summer's own ability. When she opened her eyes, a burst of emerald power silently shot out from her in all directions, blasting away the canvas covers and leaving behind thousands of blooming flowers, tall, lush hedges and trees laden with ripe peaches, apples, lemons and pears.

Summer's jaw dropped as she saw everything had been restored exactly as she remembered it from childhood. Suddenly she felt ashamed for having ridiculed the entity in its doll form.

I don't know what to say.

Marie always loved her gardens, the Tablet said. *So did you. So did I. And I am not creepy. I have never had a body. I have only borrowed them.*

Summer felt the entity retreat, and gave her mates a wry look.

"Did you hear all that?" When they both nodded, she said, "I didn't know it had feelings."

"We'll be more, ah, considerate of it in the future," Troy said.

Michael shook his head. "I still think the doll was weird."

They walked around the gardens as Summer pointed out her favorite blooms, and Marie's artful way of arranging the colors of her gardens. When they reached the huge rabbit topiary Jean-Paul had sculpted for her, trimmed exactly as he would have done, Summer almost broke down in tears.

"What's in that enclosure over there?" Troy asked as they circled back to the house.

Summer looked over at the stone and brick walls forming a long rectangular box.

"That's the walled garden where my parents always performed the seasonal rituals. Jean-Paul used a ward to retain the heat and keep the plants alive all year long, the way he did with the Monet garden on the farm." She chuckled. "And since Maman liked to perform her rituals sky-clad, it probably kept them comfortable, too."

Michael exchanged an odd look with Troy before he said, "If the tablet can restore your mother's gardens so exactly, then it can do the same for your father's manor, and the farm."

Summer nodded. "It could probably also raise the Titanic, straighten the Leaning Tower of Pisa, and enslave every mortal on this planet to serve us. That's the thing with guarding unimaginable power. Just because you can, doesn't mean you should."

"And if we rebuilt Beaumont Manor, the Templars would just blow it up again," Troy said. "I'd get bored with ruling the world, by the way. Too much paperwork."

For a moment Michael looked as if he wanted to argue, and then he nodded.

"Sometimes I still think like a Templar."

"Well, I think this is the best birthday present I've ever received," she declared and took her lovers by the hands. "However, I seem to remember a promise made me in a dream that hasn't been kept."

Michael glanced at Troy, and then spun Summer around and scooped her off her feet.

"You see to the doors," the big man said.

The dark warlock trotted ahead of them, opening and closing doors as Michael whisked her back upstairs to the master bedroom.

"We don't have any marshmallows," Troy said as he lit the candles and fireplace. "We'll have to find some other way to amuse ourselves."

"Many other ways," Michael said as he tugged off Summer's clothes. "As promised."

Drawing back the coverlet and folding it down to the foot of the bed, Summer indulged in a childish impulse and flung herself onto the mattress. The new sheets were not as soft as Marie's had been, and the pillows felt much fluffier. There was no dip in the springs from Jean-Paul's heavy body, nor the crystal carafe of water her mother always kept on the bedside table. Summer was glad of the differences. It made this her bed to share with her mates. She glanced up and remembered something that made her smile a little.

"Troy, would you take the tie-backs off those two curtains and bring them to me?" When he did she looped them at opposite sides of the canopy's cross bars and knotted the ends. "They were always tied like this on the bed."

Michael reached up to test them with a tug, and then grinned at her.

"Do you know why?"

Summer slipped her hands in the loops and held them as she wrapped her legs around his waist.

"I didn't know then, but I think I do now: leverage." As Troy came up behind her, she rubbed her bare bottom against him. "And access."

Their playfulness soon turned passionate as Summer surrendered to the magic of her mates' strong, questing hands. Troy kissed her from the small of her back to her nape and back again, parting her bottom to rub his tongue against her still-sensitive rosebud. Michael played with her breasts, watching her face as he used his mouth and fingers to gently tease and then arouse her.

Holding onto the looped tie-backs prevented Summer from returning the attention, and when she released them and fell back against Troy, Michael reared up over her, plunging into her slick pussy with a lusty stroke. The dark warlock shifted to the side and brought her hand to his rampant cock. She curled her fingers around his shaft and stroked the swelling girth.

On top of her Michael eased out and back in, moving so slowly Summer groaned in protest.

"You will like this," he told her softly.

Troy brought his free hand up to hold Summer's aching breast, and worked her pebbly nipple between his thumb and finger, squeezing and tugging it at the same time.

"Michael wants to fuck you for hours," he murmured to her. "The way he imagined he would when he was a Templar, watching you in Central Park. The fantasies he had would blow your mind."

"I wanted to take you, but not to the priory," Michael said, his voice dropping to an octave so deep Summer felt it vibrating in her bones. Sweat streaked down the sides of his face and darkened his hair from blond to dark gold as he forged even deeper inside her. "I imagined keeping you in my apartment, and feeding you, and caring for you, until you wanted me just as much. Until you came to my bed one night and took off your clothes and slipped under the sheets with me. So I could have you like this."

"Oh, Michael," Summer murmured. She had always known he'd wanted her from the first time he'd seen her, but his erotic longings stirred her own. "I felt the same for you. When you brought me to Troy, I wanted to beg you to let me stay."

Michael bent over to press his brow against her breast. "I hated to let you go, but I liked seeing you with Troy. I knew he would give you what I couldn't."

"And I did," Troy said. He caught her hand on the upstroke and held it over the engorged dome of his cockhead. "Remember, love?"

Through their link their memories merged, and Summer heard Michael groan as he experienced them for the first time.

"He likes to see you taking me," she murmured to Troy. "He has since the first time he dreamt of us together."

Michael shuddered, his big body tensing as a deep, heartfelt groan rumbled out of his chest. The pulses of his jetting semen bathed her pussy in silky warmth, triggering a small orgasm that expanded suddenly and blazed through her, a wildfire of sensation that made her cry out.

Michael rolled with her, placing her back against his front, and spreading her thighs as Troy came over them.

"I will be your bed this time," he murmured against her hair.

Troy fitted his throbbing cock against her wet opening, and slowly came into her, his eyes darkening as he felt Michael's seed engulf him along with her satiny softness.

"I can pull out before I come," he said to her, his jaw tight.

Summer understood what he meant. The mingling of their seed inside her might make her pregnant. Although she'd thought she wasn't ready to try to conceive again, the thought of her mates giving her another child made her heart swell.

"Give me all of you," she told him, lifting her hips to thrust back at him. "I won't take anything less."

Love and desire poured into her as Troy glided

in and out of her, stroking and pumping with such deep, stirring vigor that she came again, bathing him in the sweet bliss. Michael's hands covered her breasts, strong and sure as he caressed her with sensual circles of his palms. As her climax settled into quaking aftershocks, Troy bent to kiss her lips, whispering his love to her as he drove harder and fast, fucking her as if their bodies were dancing instead of moving. He came with a low cry, and her sex clasped him as he swelled and pumped his jets into her core. The last spurt sent a thrill through her as she felt his seed blend with Michael's, but this time the tingling warmth merely rippled out before it faded.

Summer didn't want to tell her lovers that there would be no child from this beautiful night, but through the link they felt her pang of regret.

"When it's time, and it's right, it will happen," Troy said to her, as he gently withdrew from her and shifted to Michael's side. "Until it does, we can practice."

Her golden warrior turned her over, and tucked her head under his chin. "Every night."

CHAPTER FOURTEEN

MORNING FILTERED INTO the kitchen, caressing Summer's face as she put the kettle on and stretched lazily. The sense of being home at last felt as warm and wonderful as the sweet, warm ache from making love last night. Smiling as she went to hunt through the pantry for the instant coffee and tea bags they'd bought in town, Summer wondered if they might have the chance to make a real home here. Both Michael and Troy loved her enough to build it. No one knew about it, and the Templars would never suspect she'd come back to live on an estate they'd burned to the ground.

Was it the right place for them to make a home for the daughter they would have someday? Summer had been happy here as a little girl, but as she'd grown older the isolation had grown almost unbearable.

She pushed aside the too-serious thoughts and considered what to have for breakfast. After last night the men would be hungry, so she'd make some hearty omelets, sausage and toast for them, and cut up some fresh fruit to have with her croissants.

The ringing of her cell phone chimed softly, and she went to retrieve it from her purse. On the display she saw Raelyn's number, and smiled.

"Hey, girl, what's going on?"

"Raelyn is dead," a trembling voice said in a tone barely above a whisper. "I found this phone in her pocket after he tortured her to death. He's drugged the dwarf, and I think he intends to kill him, too. You have to help us, Summer."

"Lorena?" Rage and dread bloomed in her chest, and her fingers tightened on the phone. "Where are you?"

"Montreal. He locked us in a room at a club called Club Chaînes," Lorena said. "Help us, Summer."

Sweat broke out on Summer's brow even as she realized something was wrong with this, something she couldn't understand. Then she recalled where she was.

"I'm too far away, Lorena. It will take hours for

me to drive back to Montreal. I need to get Troy and Michael, but the Templars are watching all the roads."

"Use the power of the Emerald Tablet," the High Priestess begged, sobbing now. "You know it can bring you here in a heartbeat. Please, Summer, I can hear him coming."

A blood-chilling howl of pain burst in Summer's ear, so loud that it was painful. Power surged inside Summer as terror and fury whirled inside her head.

Take me to Club Chaînes in Montreal. Take me to Theo and Lorena.

Verdant light curtained around her, and the kitchen flew away from her as she sailed through a blur of time and places. Just as suddenly the light vanished, and she dropped onto a stainless steel floor.

Summer hoisted herself up on her feet, jerking around as she tried to see.

"Where are you?" she said.

Glaring white LED lights switched on, blinding her. Something stabbed into her neck. Though she tried to swat it away, a pair of handcuffs were slapped on her wrist. As the drugs spread a numbing sensation through Summer, she was dragged over to an X-shaped table and restrained.

"How delightfully prompt you are," said a woman's voice. She appeared over her, looking a little drunk as she stroked her fingers across Summer's cheek. She wore a skin-tight scarlet satin jumpsuit with a matching lace mask over her face. "But we should dispense with my disguise, I think, as well as the terrible feelings that brought you here." She removed her mask.

"Lorena," Summer gasped.

"I did mention that my ability works even over a phone line, didn't I?"

She cupped Summer's breast and squeezed.

The soul-wrenching terror and thoughtless rage faded from Summer's mind, leaving her feeling thick and leaden from the sedative. She ignored the way the other woman was fondling her.

"What have you done to Theo?"

"Why, not a thing, darling. He's probably still touring the southern country with my little runaway who, I'm happy to report, is not dead. Oh, you poor girl. I lied about everything. I do that quite a lot, you know." Lorena bared her teeth in a horribly gleeful grin as she twisted Summer's nipple. "But then, payback is a witch." Summer cried out, which only delighted Lorena more. "My new Templar bitch is waiting outside. You've already met."

The arsonist was here? Summer looked up at the woman who had helped her rescue her mates, and tried to fathom why she would ally herself with such a brutal killer.

"You're confused, aren't you?" Lorena stroked her hair back from her face. "We have history that is longer than you know. Our mothers became best friends through Artemis. They did everything together. Then my father fell in love, and abandoned us. He left a letter for my mother, telling her that he had never loved her. He wrote that if he hadn't wasted his life on us, he might have had the woman he truly loved." She bent closer and whispered, "Guess who that was."

As she remembered the first time she'd met Fabiola, and the hatred in her eyes, Summer felt her stomach clench.

"Now this next part is what your mother told mine," Lorena said and patted Summer's cheek. "So listen closely. Marie said my father came to her, and begged her to take him as her third mate. When she refused, he tried to rape her, and in self-defense, she killed him." Lorena straightened. "My mother didn't believe any of it. She knew Marie had seduced my father, and then discarded him. She read the cards for Marie, in front of the entire coven, and it showed her fate. The cards showed my mother killing yours in vengeance."

Summer didn't take her eyes off the High Priestess as she reached through her mind link to Troy and Michael, but the drug had done its work.

"Marie disappeared that night, and for the next twenty-five years, we waited, and watched. We didn't find her, but we found you." The High Priestess smirked. "You were photographed at your university graduation, pretty girl, and your name was printed in the paper. Then it was just a matter of talking to your friends at school. Dear, sweet Summer, who always went home to her mother's house on holidays, and brought back sweets for her roommate from one of the candy shops in town. As soon as my mother knew where Marie was, she contacted the Templars and told them exactly where to find her. So the promise of vengeance was kept."

Summer called to the Emerald Tablet, but the entity did not respond. It had warned her in the dream garden that drugs would do this. Her own power could do nothing to protect her…unless…

The High Priestess backed away from Summer and lifted her hands, casting her psychic web around her.

"Now you will be rid of the power you have always hated. You will give it to me, Genevieve.

You will give it to me *now*."

Summer poured all her remaining energy into her natural ability, and sent it to every organic object in the room. Something deep in her mind sent a surge of power behind it, and suddenly things began to erupt from the cheap carpeting, the drapes, the walls and Lorena's clothing. Tree limbs punched through the drywall as they sprouted from the wall studs. Cotton shrubs shot up from the floor, their spiked brown bolls flowering with white balls of fluff. Vines with purple flax flowers tumbled down from the drapes.

"Stop it," Lorena screamed, slapping at the sharp bolls ripping through her jumpsuit from the cotton sprouting in her underwear.

Someone shoved the door open, and locked it behind him. Summer turned her heavy head to see a man removing a zippered leather hood.

Trapped in the plants that Summer had summoned, Lorena gaped at him.

"Bûcher? Where is–"

"Your new Templar bitch?" He grinned and glanced at Summer, then showed her the possession grimoire. "Oddly enough, once our agreement was done, he didn't want to stay." A look of distaste came over his face. "By the way, you may call me Temple Master."

As Lorena struggled, Summer's eyes widened. The High Priestess had thought to lure her to a trap, but had been caught in one as well.

The Temple Master laughed. "But soon enough you will call me Grand Master." He opened the grimoire in his hands and began to read a spell in a language so ancient it barely resembled speech. "*Knr, rnk, jthdr, rdhtj, ittak, katti.*" He droned on for another minute before he closed the book, tucked it under his arm, and pointed at Summer and Lorena. He then uttered a long series of fluid sounds. "*Aelleaelleaellea.*"

The walls shook as two small, glowing orange spheres appeared in the center of the room. They grew larger and brighter until they were the size of baseballs, and then flew away from each other, striking Lorena and Summer in the face.

The light filled Summer's skull, making her scream as she felt a horrible wrenching sensation. It burned through her mind and dragged at it, ripping and tearing until something inside her broke free. Then she flew into complete darkness, slamming back into her head so hard she nearly fainted.

Opening her eyes, Summer felt a stinging sensation around her hips, and looked down to see torn scarlet satin and blooming cotton bolls. Pale red hair flew in her face as she jerked around to see herself still restrained to the platform, her opal eyes wide as she stared back. She lifted her hand to her face, and then stared in horror at Lorena's hand.

She was no longer in her own body.

The Temple Master had put her in Lorena's body.

He walked up to her, catching her as her knees buckled.

"Welcome to your new prison, Ms. Lautner."

• • • • •

The End of *Burned*

• • • • •

Summer's story continues in *Reclaimed (Book Ten of the Silver Wood Coven Series)*.

For a sneak peek, turn the page.

Reclaimed (Book Ten of the Silver Wood Coven Series)
Excerpt

After taking a shower Troy Atwater tugged on his trousers, and went to open the violet and gold damask curtains. Thin, early morning light illuminated the master bedroom. Tiny rainbows danced on his damp, bare chest from the prismatic crystals hung in the window as he surveyed the lush, blooming gardens beyond the house. Summer Lautner's formidable magic had created spring in the midst of winter, but it was her presence that made the world seem to brim with renewal. He knew her love had dissolved the frustration and anger and bitter determination that he'd brought with him on this journey. He felt strong and calm for the first time since coming to Canada.

"It is good that you are feeling powerful, Pagan," Michael Charbon said as he rolled out of the oversize bed. The big man scrubbed a huge hand over his shaggy golden hair.

"Because if you used all the hot water again, I will beat you senseless."

"That's what you get for bonding with a water elemental, Paladin." Troy took the towel from around his neck and tossed it at his sentinel brother, who stopped in mid-stretch to catch it. "Besides, after last night, you need a cold shower."

The big man glanced up at two curtain tie-backs hanging from the canopy.

"It was worth it." He retreated into the bathroom.

Troy went to the suitcases to retrieve some clean clothes, his mouth hitching as he picked up on some of Michael's thoughts from the shower. Being mated to the Guardian of the Emerald Tablet, the oldest and most powerful grimoire in the world, had plenty of advantages beyond their telepathic link. Their lady contained all the Tablet's magic in her mind, which made her the most powerful Wiccan on the planet. It also made her completely unique among witches.

Not only was Summer beautiful and kind, as

a lover she was deeply passionate and wickedly sensual.

Troy touched a love bite on his neck and smiled a little. Since he and Michael were very physical, demanding lovers an ordinary woman might have had trouble accommodating them both. But Summer's bloodline produced extraordinarily strong and resilient females who always took two mates. They also gave birth to only one daughter, who was fated to become the next Guardian—a daughter conceived with two fathers.

A familiar pang of sorrow jolted his heart as he thought of the baby they'd lost.

When Summer had miscarried their child while preventing a horrific car accident, Troy had been outraged that the Emerald Tablet hadn't prevented it. The accident had made Summer decide to return to Canada to explore the two estates her fathers had left to her, but Troy knew how desperate his lady had been to escape all the reminders of their loss. The misery she'd suffered had made him hell-bent on separating the Tablet from her.

Since coming to Montreal they had been drawn into dangerous intrigues with Artemis Coven, the all-female group to which Summer's mother Marie had once belonged. Discovering a Templar priory hidden in the city had resulted in Summer being hunted again for her powers. They'd also attracted the notice of a crazed arsonist who had been cursed by Marie, and who had come close to killing Summer twice. But instead of devoting himself to protecting his lady, Troy's determination to end her guardianship by any means necessary had alienated Michael, and had nearly torn apart the three of them.

But Summer had brought them back together, and showed Troy how wrong he'd been. He still didn't care for the Tablet—he probably never would—but he realized now that his blind anger had left Summer vulnerable. It had nearly destroyed the love he shared with the two most important people in his life.

"I do not have to beat you senseless after all," Michael said. Steam wafted into the bedroom as he emerged, a towel around his hips. "You do a fine job of it yourself."

"Just clearing my head," Troy said, as he tugged on a sea-blue sweater, and shook out his thick mane of black hair. "I want to start over, with Summer, and you, and everything."

"Think about something happier," the big man suggested. "Like last night."

Troy sighed. "We might have gotten her pregnant again, you know. Me coming inside her after you like that."

Due to the unusual nature of her bloodline, in order for their lady to conceive they both had to fill her with their seed.

Michael grunted as he went to the suitcase to grab some clothes.

"She told you to, and you wanted to. She knew what might happen, but she needed you."

Troy chuckled. "Well, there is that. You didn't seem to mind playing mattress for us."

"I feel what you feel, and it was erotic. I almost came again while you were pumping inside her." He pulled on a pair of corduroys. "She went crazy for it, too, the way you gave it to her. She likes it when you go deep and fast.

Me she likes slow, and hard."

Troy didn't have a qualm about sharing Summer with Michael. The nature of their bond made jealousy impossible. They had no sexual interest in each other, but they both worked together perfectly to assure their lady's pleasure. Summer would probably be surprised by how often they talked about it, but that, too, was part of the bond they had as her mates.

"You think too much about it," Michael added. "But at least you do not do that in bed."

"I couldn't stop myself," Troy admitted. "I loved how she felt inside. Gods, she was like wet satin, and so hot for it. Remember those sounds she made? Every time I plowed into her she gripped me like a fist. We need to do that again."

Michael chuckled. "We will. We promised her sex every night, and I think Beauty will hold us to that." He grimaced and reached down to adjust the swelling bulge under his shorts before zipping up his pants. "I hope she does."

"She might like sex every morning, too," Troy said and glanced at the empty bed. "After breakfast, we'll coax her back up here."

"I like the coaxing," the big man said and stroked a thumb across his lower lip. "Or we can have her for breakfast. Undress her, and use the kitchen table. She might be a little sore after last night, so…"

Troy smothered a groan as Michael's carnal thoughts came pouring into his mind.

"We'll take turns kissing her pussy," Troy suggested. He heard the whistle of the kettle downstairs. "Come on, we'd better hurry, or she'll be too busy cooking. I want her more than food."

MORE BOOKS BY HAZEL HUNTER

SILVER WOOD COVEN SERIES

Though she's taken the name given her by a kind stranger, Summer can no more explain waking up homeless and covered in blood, than she can the extreme attraction drawing people to her. Amnesiac, confused, and frightened, she's not even aware that she's a witch. But help arrives in two very different forms: the cool and restrained Templar Michael Charbon and his centuries-long friend Wiccan Major Troy Atwater.

Rescued (Silver Wood Coven Book One)

Stolen (Silver Wood Coven Book Two)

United (Silver Wood Coven Book Three)

Betrayed (Silver Wood Coven Book Four)

Revealed (Silver Wood Coven Book Five)

Silver Wood Coven Box Set (Books 1 - 5)

Lost (Silver Wood Coven Book Six)

Divided (Silver Wood Coven Book Seven)

Gone (Silver Wood Coven Book Eight)

Burned (Silver Wood Coven Book Nine)

Reclaimed (Silver Wood Coven Book Ten)

Sign up for my newsletter to be notified of new releases!

THE FOREVER FAIRE SERIES

She's found a magical lover. But is he real? Kayla Rowe and her little sister are running for their lives. Chased from town to town by a gang of bikers that no one else sees, Kayla is down to her last dollar and out of ideas. But when she stumbles into the winter camp of a man who is larger than life, her world changes.

Hunted (Forever Faire Book One)

Outcast (Forever Faire Book Two)

Hidden (Forever Faire Book Three)

Denied (Forever Faire Book Four)

Destined (Forever Faire Book Five)

THE SANCTUARY COVEN SERIES

An innocent, young woman. A single-minded warlock. A web of seduction that ensnares them both. Life is finally starting to work out for Heather Moore: a place all her own, a fulfilling career, and a wonderful new man in her life. Straight from the pages of a magazine, her French lover is the stuff of dreams. Strong and sexy, considerate and funny, it's as though she's been waiting from him all her short life.

Twice Seduced (Sanctuary Coven Book One)

Taken Together (Sanctuary Coven Book Two)

Matched Mates (Sanctuary Coven Book Three)

Primal Partners (Sanctuary Coven Book Four)

Forever Joined (Sanctuary Coven Book Five)

Sanctuary Coven Box Set (Books 1 - 5)

THE HOLLOW CITY COVEN SERIES

A daring quest. A deadly enemy. A protector who won't quit. Although Wiccan Gillian Granger's life's work is finding a legendary city, her research in musty libraries hasn't prepared her for the field, let alone a gorgeous escort. Shayne Savatier knows he's on a milk run, especially after he meets his beautiful charge. But when enemies attack her, everything changes. Passion intertwines with protection, and duty bonds hard with desire.

Possessed (Hollow City Coven Book One)

Shadowed (Hollow City Coven Book Two)

Trapped (Hollow City Coven Book Three)

Haunted (Hollow City Coven Book Four)

Remembered (Hollow City Coven Book Five)

Reborn (Hollow City Coven Book Six)

Hollow City Coven Box Set (Books 1 - 6)

THE CASTLE COVEN SERIES

Novice witch Hailey Devereaux had resolved to live life as an outsider. Possessed of a unique Wiccan ability, her own people shun her. But that all ends when two very different men enter her life: the brooding Major Kieran McCallen and Coven Master Piers Dayton. But their training and tests are only the beginning. As she struggles to fulfill her destiny and find her place

in the world, Hailey also discovers love.

Found (Castle Coven Book One)

Abandoned (Castle Coven Book Two)

Healed (Castle Coven Book Three)

Claimed (Castle Coven Book Four)

Imprisoned (Castle Coven Book Five)

Sacrificed (Castle Coven Book Six)

Castle Coven Box Set (Books 1 - 6)

THE MAGUS CORPS SERIES

Meet the warlocks of the Magus Corps, sworn

to protect Wiccans at all costs. As they find and

track fledgling witches, it's a race against an

ancient enemy that would rather see all Wiccans

dead. But where danger and intimacy come

together, passion is never far behind.

Dominic (Her Warlock Protector Book 1)

Sebastian (Her Warlock Protector Book 2)

Logan (Her Warlock Protector Book 3)

Colin (Her Warlock Protector Book 4)

Vincent (Her Warlock Protector Book 5)

Jackson (Her Warlock Protector Book 6)

Trent (Her Warlock Protector Book 7)

Her Warlock Protector Box Set (Books 1 - 7)

THE SECOND SIGHT SERIES

Join psychic Isabelle de Grey and FBI profiler

Mac MacMillan as they hunt a serial killer in the streets of Los Angeles. Even as their search closes in on the kidnapper, they discover not only clues, but a fiery passion that quickly consumes them.

Touched (Second Sight Book 1)

Torn (Second Sight Book 2)

Taken (Second Sight Book 3)

Chosen (Second Sight Book 4)

Charmed (Second Sight Book 5)

Changed (Second Sight Book 6)

Second Sight Box Set (Books 1 - 6)

THE PASSAGE TO PASSION SERIES

Travel the world in these breathless tales of erotic romance. Each features a different couple in fast-paced tales of fiery passion.

Arctic Exposure

In an Alaskan storm, a young couple cling to each for life and for love.

Desert Thirst

In the Sahara, a master tracker has the scent of his fiery client.

Jungle Fever

A forensic accountant blossoms under the care of a plantation owner in Thailand.

Mountain Wilds

A beautiful doctor on the rebound crashes with

her pilot in British Columbia.

Island Magic

Two treasure-hunting scuba divers are

kidnapped in the Caribbean.

Passage to Passion - The Complete Collection

This box set includes all five books: Arctic

Exposure, Desert Thirst, Jungle Fever, Mountain

Wilds, and Island Magic.

THE ROMANCE IN THE RUINS NOVELS

Explore the ancient world and the new in these standalone novels of erotic romance. Each features a hero and heroine who come together against all odds, in exotic and remote settings where danger and love are found in equal measure.

Words of Love

Set in the heartland of the ancient Maya.

Labyrinth of Love

Set on the ancient Greek island of Crete.

Stars of Love

Set in the rugged Pueblo Southwest.

Sign up for my newsletter to be notified of new

releases!

ENJOY THIS BOOK?

You can make a big difference.

Reviews are the most powerful tools in my arsenal when it comes to getting attention for my books. Much as I'd like to, I don't have the financial muscle of a New York publisher. I can't take out full pages ads in the newspaper or put posters on the subway.

(Not yet, anyway.)

But I do have something much more powerful and effective than that, and it's something that those publishers would kill to get their hands on.

A committed and loyal group of readers.

Honest reviews of my books help bring them to the attention of other readers.

If you've enjoyed this book I would be very grateful if you could spend just five minutes leaving a review—it can be as short as you like.

Thank you so much!

DEDICATION

For Mr. H.

Made in the USA
Coppell, TX
14 June 2020

28052182R00085